VIPER

Other books by John Desjarlais:

*Bleeder**

Relics

The Throne of Tara

*From Sophia Institute Press

JOHN DESJARLAIS

VIPER

A MYSTERY

SOPHIA INSTITUTE PRESS
Manchester, New Hampshire

Sophia Institute Press®
Box 5284, Manchester, NH 03108
1-800-888-9344
www.SophiaInstitute.com

Printed in the United States of America

This book is a work of fiction. Any resemblance to real people or situations is completely coincidental.

Library of Congress Cataloging-in-Publication Data

Desjarlais, John, 1953-
    Viper : a mystery / John J. Desjarlais.
    p. cm.
    ISBN 978-1-933184-80-7 (pbk. : alk. paper) 1. Hispanic American women —
    Fiction. 2. Murder — Investigation — Fiction. 3. Drug dealers — Fiction.
    I. Title.
PS3554.E11577V57 2011
813'.54 — dc22

                                                         2010045884

First Printing

VIPER

PROLOGOMENA

I will make you enemies of each other:
You, serpent, and the woman.
She will crush your head
And you will strike at her heels.

Genesis 3:15

CHAPTER 1

Selena De La Cruz finish-welded the high-flow exhaust tubes at the manifold flanges, twisted off the white flame, and lifted the mask to inspect her work. *Perfecto.* She blew at the torch as though it were a smoking gun and thought about the next tasks: install a low-temperature thermostat to keep the Charger's engine cool, check the brake bleeder valves, and — line one on the garage phone trilled.

¿Ay, ahora qué? she sighed with a roll of her eyes. Hadn't she made it clear to her new receptionist, Felicia, that her lunch hour in the insurance-claims garage was *sagrada* and she was not to be disturbed while working on her car? She ducked from under the Matco lift, tugged off her work gloves and crossed to the Formica counter, her Filas sneakers squeaking on the glossy concrete floor. She raked her fingers through her sable hair. It must be an *emergencia*, she thought, her heart rate accelerating with each quickened step. *Un accidente malo* with injuries. Lord knows how the early November drizzle had slicked the roads.

She seized the chirping phone and punched a button. "*¿Sí,* Felicia?"

"Selena? Is that really you?" asked a man's voice.

She wrinkled her brow. It wasn't her brother Francisco asking for another loan. It wasn't her brother Lorenzo looking for a place to crash, now that his wife had kicked him out again. It wasn't Reed Stubblefield, calling about their weekend date; he knew better. And it felt a bit presumptuous for an insurance-agency customer to call her by her first name. The nerve. And how did he get this direct-line number? She drew a cleansing breath and used her softest business voice. "How may I help you, sir?"

"Selena Perez, ex-DEA?"

"Who is this?"

"Geez, you don't know how hard it is to find you."

Her heart hammered against her ribs. "I'm sorry, sir, I don't know what you're talking about."

"Sure you do. But being hard to find was the whole idea, wasn't it?"

She rifled through her memory. "Del?"

"The same," Del Bragg, her old team leader said with a snort. "Say, I like your new last name. Dee-lah-Crooz?"

"From John of the Cross, a Spanish poet," she said, her breath suddenly short. "I always liked his work."

"Yeah, well, I always liked your work, too."

"That's not true. You wrote me up twice for insubordination."

"Three times. The third was because of that little girl you shot. I know you want to forget about that."

"What do you want, Del?"

"So don't thank me for getting the media off your butt about it. She lived, didn't she? Aren't you over it yet?"

"I said, what do you want?"

"Guess you're not over it, not even five years later," Bragg said. "But I need you back anyway."

"When I left the agency, it was for good," Selena said, biting off the words. "I did everything I needed to do, and I'm done. Goodbye."

"The Snake is out of prison," Bragg shot back.

Selena brought the receiver back to her ear. "No way."

"Way," Bragg said. "His lawyer finally got the appeal. The judge said there was no evidence to prove the substance he was attempting to buy from you was heroin since the state couldn't provide any chemical testing on it at the time. You remember why, don't you?"

The fire.

"He's free and back in business," Bragg continued. "We need your help to find him."

"Yeah, right," she huffed. "You'll just blow my cover and make me a target for every dopehead I ever busted. Forget it, Del."

"You blew your own cover, Selena," Bragg retorted.

"What do you mean?"

"Hang on a sec." Some paper rustled. "Here it is. I've got a *Sinnissippi Weekly Observer* newspaper clipping in front of me now, the whole story of some murder case involving a priest. You helped the River Falls police last spring, and there's your picture, big as day. You're still lookin' great. Working out, huh? Love the long hair. Hey, are you seeing this guy in the other picture — Red Stubblefeld?"

"Reed Stubblefield," she said shortly. "And it's none of your business."

"It might be. Listen up: If I can get hold of this newspaper article and recognize you and find you, anyone can, including The Snake, and believe me, I think he's looking for you."

Selena felt her forearms prickling with goose bumps.

"I can be at your house at 1500 hours to talk this over. I don't want to come to your office, since we might need you undercover again. I told your receptionist we were the police checking on somebody's ID. It wasn't a lie. Hey — you live alone?"

"Yes."

"Not surprised. Can you get the afternoon off?"

"I'm the boss."

"Still got your piece?"

"No. It was government issued. I returned it."

"I thought so. I've got another one for you. You didn't like the standard government model, though, is that right? You had a P226 Sig Sauer, wasn't it?"

"Yes." Her heart recoiled against her ribs *pow pow pow*.

"You're gonna need it," Bragg said. "You remember what he said to you on the day we busted him."

She closed her eyes. "I do."

And the images of that day flooded back.

CHAPTER 2

It was five years ago.

At that time, like every time, Selena saw right away why he called himself *La Serpiente*, The Snake.

For one thing, he wore rattlesnake-skin boots with the steel toes that Bragg and her Anglo colleagues at Drug Enforcement sneeringly called "Fence Climbers." When he crossed his sinewy legs and swung his foot, the tip glinted.

For another, his unmoving onyx eyes fixed on her cleavage — not all that uncommon when she met men — but that gaze was not measuring her size. It was calculating a striking distance. She averted her eyes to the side, a demure Mexican custom she hadn't lost through acculturation. Locking eyes is also how snakes paralyze their prey. She wouldn't give him the pleasure.

With a casual shake of her head, she quickly assessed possible escape routes. A back door. Two open windows where the greasy odor of *tamales fritos* drifted in from the outdoor *cantina*. No telling what was beyond the ratty blankets hung as partitions on laundry lines that stretched along the barracks wall. Behind them, shadows and voices. A woman's giggle. Along the opposite wall, empty bunk beds, the men away at work. It might be rural Illinois, but it looked just like the barrio back-alleys of Mexico City when she did undercover work there.

She puzzled over why The Snake arranged to meet here, in makeshift quarters for immigrant slaughterhouse workers, where the stink of hog offal clung to the men's overalls and to the army-surplus sheets. Maybe he thought its remoteness more secure against reconnaissance or a raid. He was certainly more in control, and she didn't like it.

A horse-faced *mestizo* shouldered through the partition. The man gave her a leer and then winked at her. Selena's stomach clenched in disgust. Women behind the blankets were servicing laborers, and this man thought she was one of them reporting for work. She narrowed her eyes to angry slits, and the man, intimidated, hurried to the door and ducked out.

"*Ahí nos vemos,*" The Snake rasped to the departing customer. See ya later. No doubt he would.

"I didn't know you ran a side business," Selena said, masking her revulsion. "Are the women documented?"

The Snake laughed through his teeth. It sounded like a hiss. "Does it matter?" he said. "They are fully employed, and they put food on their family's table. Maybe someday they can afford fancy shoes like yours."

We'll nail you for aiding and abetting human trafficking, too, slimeball, Selena thought, glancing around, anticipating areas of possible threat.

"I was hoping for a meeting place more private, as before," Selena said. *And more open, like a parking lot.* Less chance of being trapped or taken hostage.

"So do they," he said, waving a hand at the door where another customer arrived. *La Serpiente* shifted in his chair and smiled at him. No fangs. But the teeth were bleach white and evenly spaced like the military tombstones that paraded on both sides of her brother Antonio's grave.

"And when did you start using bodyguards?" Selena asked, lifting her chin at the stern woman and the bald goon in the V-shaped beard and black T-shirt standing beside the seated Snake. The man's hungry eyes scanned her up and down. A phone blinked in his ear. A Beretta gleamed from his belt.

"Since I could afford them," The Snake answered. "Business has been good, and when business is good, people try to take advantage of you. I'm sure you won't. Let's see what you brought for me today. But first —"

He cocked his head, a signal. "Rosita! *Búscala.*"

The copper-cheeked woman with peroxide hair and gang tattoos stepped forward to search Selena for weapons or a wire.

Selena stuck out her arms, crucifix-style. "I was already searched outside by the door guard."

The Snake smiled. "I know. I like to be sure."

Rosita circled behind her. She ran her calloused hands up Selena's black jeans, ankles to hips, rubbed her back and belly, patted her sides and chest, lingering there. When she stepped away, she whispered "Nice shoes" in Selena's ear with an envious look at her red open-toed Espadrille wedge sandals. The woman's teeth were streaked and cracked. Meth-head. It was bigger than heroin or weed in the Midwest now, smuggled across the border or made on remote farms where the ingredients were easily available. "It's in her bra," Rosita announced in a gravelly smoker's voice.

"I also keep my passport there when I travel to see The Barracuda in Oaxaca," Selena said.

The Snake leaned forward, eyes gleaming. "Did you see him last week as you promised? What does he think of my little business proposal?" he asked.

It wasn't so little. He wanted to be the Mexican cartel kingpin's Chicago — and hence Midwest — distributor.

"The fact that I'm here should tell you," Selena said.

He smiled, satisfied. "Tell me again: does he really look like a barr—"

"Yes," Selena said, jumping on the question too soon. Did it make her seem nervous? "Little teeth, always showing. Breathes through his mouth. Eyes widely set, so they look like they are on the sides of his head. He says he can see all around him and no one can take him by surprise."

"Another thing we have in common," he said, closing his eyes. The snake eyes tattooed on his eyelids made him look awake and prepared to lunge. No one would dare assassinate him in his sleep.

He opened his eyes and curled his lip, a sign that she had passed the test. Why was he testing her? Didn't he trust her after two walkaway buys, the $50,000 flashroll, the dinner and that dance with his cold hand in the small of her back?

"Here's what he has for you to sell," Selena said, slipping two fingers down her scalloped blouse and extracting the one-ounce sample. "If you do well with the first shipment, he says he will consider a partnership. You have the down payment?"

The Snake snapped his fingers, and Rosita produced a thick roll of greenbacks. She waved it in the air.

Selena flicked the baggie in The Snake's direction. The burly thug beside him snatched it in mid-flight. The man's belt creaked when he leaned over. He snapped open the ziplock bag, licked a fingertip, and dipped it in.

"*Chocolate de Fumanchú*," the bodyguard confirmed.

Low-life amateur, Selena thought. No professional tests it like that anymore. Must be watching *Miami Vice* reruns.

"I never test heroin myself," The Snake apologized, "not after what happened to Don Caballo last year in Colombia."

"Forgive me, *señor*," Selena said, "but it was Venezuela."

"Ah!" he exclaimed with palms up in mock dismay at his error. "But of course. How could I forget?"

Test two over. Something wasn't right. She held out her hand, waiting for the money.

"The poor man," *La Serpiente* said. "I've heard tell that Fortune, as they call her, is a drunken and capricious woman and, worse still, blind; and so she doesn't see what she's doing, and doesn't know whom she is casting down or raising up."

Always with the Cervantes quotes. Especially when he was edgy. *Does he suspect something? Is he provoking me with that "woman" line? Is he stalling?* "You did not forget his terms, I trust?" she said, tapping her foot.

"I remember," he said.

That was good. There was no need to belabor the details. *Get in, get out.* "Good," Selena said, extending her palm. "I'll take my payment and be on my way."

The bodyguard pressed his palm to his earpiece and then whispered something close to his boss's ear. The Snake's pupils widened. "One last thing, Selena, *mi corazón*," he said, dwelling, it seemed, on the *s* sounds.

A new condition? Test three? *Play impatient. Balk and threaten to back out.* She rested her palm on her hip. "*Sí*, what is it?"

"That truck pulling in — is it my delivery already?"

Rosita pulled back a window shade. "It's just the *Supermercado* produce delivery truck for the *cantina*."

"They already came early this morning," *La Serpiente* said, scowling. He pointed to Selena's feet. "Take off your shoes."

Madre de Dios, he knows. She shook a finger at him, irritated. "*¿Qué cochinada es esta?* Give me the money now or the deal is off."

"The shoes, *por favor*."

The bodyguard drew his Beretta.

Aimed at her.

She kicked off her shoes.

The door splintered open. The room blazed white, and the blast from the Magnum 470 flash grenade hurled Selena to the floor.

"Police! Search warrant!" Del Bragg bellowed. "Down on the floor! Down! Down!" The agents behind him, in helmets and Kevlar armor, rushed in and dropped to their trained positions. Selena sprawled on the planks, covering her head. The Snake's bodyguard squeezed two shots into the air before Bragg did a Rambo-roll and unloaded fifteen rounds from his M-4 into him. Cartridges flew. Hot grenade shards skittered across the floor. Women shrieked "*¡La migra! ¡La migra!*" as the fabric of the hanging blankets crackled into flames and smoke filled the room.

Rosita, on hands and knees, grabbed Selena's sandals and scrambled for the back door. An officer yelled at her to halt. She shook a shoe at him in scorn. He mistook it for a pistol. He pumped five deafening rounds into her.

The snapping fire raced across the blankets and leaped to the walls like a ravenous animal. Wailing women stumbled outside, sheets to their breasts, kerchiefs over their mouths and noses. Agents coughed despite their masks, hauling men outside with their arms twisted behind them, shouting in badly accented Spanish.

Bragg seized Selena by the arm, yanked her to her feet, and hauled her outside. Once in the open, he jerked her arm up behind her to the middle of her back and shoved her toward the supermarket truck, barking, "You are under arrest. You have the right to remain silent —"

"Not so hard, Del," Selena said through gritted teeth. "You're hurting me."

"Gotta make it look real, dollface," he grunted in her ear. He resumed his mock arrest. "Anything you say can and will be used against you in a court of law. You have the right to an attorney —"

Bragg pushed her past The Snake who was belly-down in the dirt with an officer's boot in the small of his back and with his head jerked up by the hair. Another agent waved a search warrant in his grimacing face.

"This is your fault, Selena!" The Snake hissed. "I'll get you for this!"

"It's your fault!" she screamed at him. "¡Puerco! Pig!"

"¡Puta! Whore! ¡Traidora!" he spat back.

"Shut up," the officer said, and rammed his M16 stock into his ribs.

The paddy wagons screeched up, although at a farther distance than planned. The barracks were engulfed now. Smoke billowed from the windows and long tongues of flame licked the tarpaper roof, spitting an acrid smell.

"Get these rats out of here!" Bragg ordered, still gripping Selena's wrist like a vise below her shoulder blade. "Let the others go. We got what we came for. And get those pickup trucks out of the way before the gas tanks blow."

"Local fire on their way, sir," an agent called with a phone to his ear.

"Good." He pushed Selena behind the delivery truck and released her.

She rubbed her throbbing elbow, took two steps and dropped to one knee, gulping for fresh air. Nausea writhed in her belly.

Bragg stripped off his helmet and face mask. "You all right, Selena?"

"Sure, Del."

She wasn't. She fought off dizziness.

"Let me get you some water."

Selena wiped bitter spit from her mouth. She watched Bragg open the truck cabin's creaking door and toss his helmet on the seat. She tried to swallow, but her throat burned from stomach acid and smoke. She levered up, steadied herself against the truck, and faced the Quonset hut barracks that were now completely consumed in flames. The blurry heat prickled her cheeks.

That was a close call. Too close.

She back-fisted the truck in anger. The evidence was burning. Maybe the recording would be enough. They might have gotten him for prostitution or human trafficking if Del had detained the women. Not our jurisdiction, he'd say. That's for the ICE guys or the FBI. *Gringo idiota.*

Bragg twisted off the cap of a water bottle and handed it to her. She took an eager mouthful, rinsed, and spat.

"You know what I think?" Bragg chortled. "I think he wasn't interested in the sample at all. He wanted to hold you hostage. To see what you were worth to The Barracuda. He didn't know about the mic in the shoes. He just wanted to keep you from running away. He was probably going to ask for your clothes next. Don't thank me for busting in a little early."

"Fine, I won't," she said, wiping her mouth.

"We got everything. The mic in the shoes worked good."

She squinted at the roiling flames.

"I liked those shoes," she said.

15

CHAPTER 3

Selena slipped into the faux leopard slingbacks and examined the fall of her pinstriped pantsuit leg over them in the hallway mirror when the doorbell chimed promptly at 1500 hours. She brushed away a little excess powder from the corner of her sienna eyes and primped her mouth, the lip liner two shades darker than the magenta gloss to match her caramel complexion. *Always dress so you will not be mistaken for the help, mija,* she heard her mother saying. But no makeup could ever soften the Aztec hatchet of a nose buried in the middle of her face. She leaned to the peephole from the side, an old precaution, and hitched her breath.

She never expected to see Del Bragg with a priest in tow. But there beside him on the front stoop stood a stout cleric wearing a Roman collar, a rumpled raincoat turned up against a spitting drizzle, a silver halo of hair, and a cherubic smile. Complete with a folded umbrella at his side, he might have been G. K. Chesterton's Father Brown. She opened the door.

"*Buenos días, Señorita Selena,*" the priest said with a courteous bow. Panamanian accent. But he didn't look Latin at all, not with those rosy cheeks. "I'm Father Johnny Sullivan, the new pastor at Saint Mary's parish," he said. "Glad to finally meet you. I've heard a lot about you."

She returned the greeting with the little curtsey her godmother taught her to do when meeting a man of the cloth. "How do you do, Father?" she said, ill at ease.

"Hey, Selena," Bragg said, ogling her up and down with his ice-blue eyes. "How the heck are ya?"

"Del, you haven't changed," she said.

Still muscular in his fifties, in a sport jacket too small for him beneath an open trench coat, he stood off to the side, chest out, facing her shoulder to shoulder at a safe distance, as agents are trained to do. He kept his leg stance wide with the gun-side foot back for balance. He carried a briefcase, not the usual M-4 he cradled when approaching someone's front door.

"You neither," Bragg said. "Still into the shoes, huh?"

She lifted her three-inch heel for a full effect. "Giuseppi Zanottis."

Bragg tugged up his trouser leg. "Sears Roebucks. Can we come in now? It's cold out here."

"Sure." She swung the door fully open.

"Nice place," Bragg said, elbowing past her and lifting his square jaw to survey the living room, as though searching it. "You sure you don't share it with what's-his-name — Steve?"

"Reed," she corrected him. "And no, he has his own place in Chicago. He stays in his brother's three-season hunting cabin when he's visiting out here."

"See, Padre?" Bragg said, shrugging off his coat. "I told you she was clean as they come."

The priest dropped his umbrella into the hallway stand. "I hope this isn't a bad time for you," he said while Selena gathered their coats.

"Not at all," she said. But was it ever a good time when a priest showed up unannounced at the door with an officer? The last time it happened, a spit-polished sergeant held his hat to his heart and announced *We regret to inform you that Antonio —*"

"Naturally, you must wonder why I'm here," the cleric continued. "I'm sorry if my presence has alarmed you. *Perdóneme, por favor.*"

"There is nothing to forgive," Selena assured him, feeling the heat in her neck. Priests were better than cops at reading faces. She indicated seats in the living room, dropped coats in the study, and offered coffee. No one wanted any.

"Mr. Bragg thought it best for me to come to explain things firsthand, myself," Father Sullivan offered, settling into the couch and eyeing the collection of framed *santos* and *virgencitas* cluttering the end table.

"I thought this was about The Snake," Selena said.

"Yeah, Selena, it is, partly," Bragg said. "But something's been happening at Reverend Johnny's church that may be connected to The Snake. Go ahead, Padre."

The priest steepled his fingers. "You are familiar, I imagine, with *El Día de Los Muertos*? The Day of the Dead?"

"Of course," Selena replied. "Major Mexican holiday, November 2. My family always made a memorial altar in the house for our ancestors. My mother, aunts, and godmother spent days baking sweet breads and making the marigold garlands for it."

She decided not to mention she still kept the *tradición*. In the spare bedroom upstairs, she had set up the annual shrine with framed photos of her mother, her father, and her brother Antonio set on fringed linen, surrounded by potted mums, white votive candles, and a tray of sweetbreads and sourdough *pan de muerto*. She'd left a trail of marigolds from Antonio's grave to her home to help him find his way, as her mother made her promise to do.

"Then you also know of The Book of the Deceased kept in the church?"

"Same as the Book of the Dead, right?" Selena asked. "The ledger put out before All Souls' Day where people write the names of relatives who have passed away so they can be prayed for? Sure. I write in my mother's and brother's names every year." *Ever since Antonio died in that car accident in Germany. Drugs. Always drugs. Where was God then, Father?* "So what does this have to do with The Snake?"

"He's coming to that," Bragg said. He fidgeted. His shoulder holster bulged against his blazer.

"I did not recognize some of the names written in the church's Book of the Deceased," the priest said, "since I have been here only since August, when Father Brian retired. You knew him?"

"Yes," she replied. "And Father Ray."

The priest shook his head. "A very strange case. You had a part in it?"

She held up her thumb and index finger, nearly pinched. "*Un poquito.*" Just a little.

Bragg inspected his fingernails. "Can we get on to this case?"

"*No hay ninguna prisa, Padre,*" Selena said quietly. "*Tome su tiempo.*" There's no need to hurry. Take your time.

Bragg wrinkled his nose, annoyed as usual when Selena spoke Spanish in his presence. He'd never bothered to learn more than *show your hands*, *get down*, and *you're under arrest*.

"I read the police report in the newspaper and the obituaries religiously," the priest continued, forcing a little smile. "Very unhappily, that is how I often learn someone in the parish is in trouble with the authorities. I noticed that some names in the newspaper were names in the Book of the Deceased."

He stopped. Looked for a reaction.

Selena tilted her head. "What's so unusual about that?"

"The names in the newspaper — names of men who were murdered — appeared in the Book of the Deceased *before* they were dead."

Bragg butt in. "Put another way, when the names were written in the book, they weren't dead yet."

"Are you sure they are the same men?" Selena questioned. "Latino names can be — well, so similar. And undocumented immigrants use many different names to stay hidden."

"I am aware of that," the priest said. "But I noticed that the men turned up dead in the exact same order they were listed in the book. That's when I went to the police about it."

"That's how I got involved," Bragg said. "County sheriff's department ran a HUMP card for each name and that generated a ViCAP alert in our office since the names matched ones in our database. As soon as I checked AFIS to confirm identities, I called the locals."

The priest gave a little shrug and a smile. "I'm afraid I don't speak your language."

"Sorry, Father," Selena said. "He means that Sheriff's deputies filled out a form with the names and submitted them to an FBI computer database called the Violent Criminal Apprehension Program.

It looks for patterns in unsolved homicides, to see if any are connected. Agent Bragg checked the names with the FBI's Automated Fingerprint Identification System."

"And that's how I knew for sure nearly everyone listed in that book had a run-in with The Snake at some point. You know: an enforcer makes off with a stash for his private use, a runner turns into an informant. Sheesh, I paid them better than he did."

"It's a hit list," Selena whispered.

"Looks like it," Bragg continued, brow lowered, unaccustomed to being interrupted. "Clearly, he's peeved, although why he'd warn them in advance of a hit and give them time to scoot is beyond me."

"It intimidates them and enhances his reputation," Selena said. "And they prove how *macho* they are by staying, not running. No *Latino* would lose face that way. So who is on the list?"

"I brought the book," Bragg said, bending to his briefcase. "You'll recognize the names. Here, put these gloves on."

Selena tugged on the cotton gloves as Bragg lifted out a plastic evidence bag holding a cloth-bound book. It looked like an oversize accountant's ledger, hunter green with a tan leather trim. Selena took the labeled bag, unzipped it, slid the book out, and laid it across her lap. She pinched the black satin bookmark and opened to that page.

The left side for the previous year was filled with two columns of handwritten names below a stylized Old Testament Scripture passage: *"Precious in the sight of the Lord is the death of His saints."* On the right side, the current year's names were penned, by different hands, below a New Testament verse: *"Jesus Christ is the firstborn of the dead."*

Selena traced her index finger down the list. Along the way were family names in groups of three or four, bearing the same surnames — deceased parents, grandparents, siblings: James Fletcher. Esther Fletcher. Toby Fletcher. Sam Millard. Sadie Millard. Sandy Millard. Henry, George, and Vivian Castlebaum. Jan Stemke. Laura Stemke. Everett Wilson. Then there were the last nine names, all Latino, all

different. They were scrawled in the same aggressive majuscule with
oversize capitals.

Victor Velásquez
JJ García
Pinky Lee Hernández
Juan José López
Franky Rodríguez
Roberto Batista
Eddie Castro
Oscar Orozco

"Now you see why you need to be part of this," Bragg said.
Selena bit her lower lip as a chill slithered up her spine.
The last name in the list was hers.

CHAPTER 4

She tapped the name with her fingertip. "Selena Peña," she said. "The fake ID he knew me by. So it's him for sure."

"He might know your new last name, from that newspaper story," Bragg said, "which may explain why the list is in Father Johnny's church. You're the last name, so he puts the list in this town, his last stop on his revenge tour."

"But," asked the priest, "why not use the new name?"

Selena wrinkled her brow. "It could be his way saying, 'I know who you were, and who you are.' "

"So he knows *where* you are, too," Bragg said.

"I've got an unlisted number and a post-office box," she said.

"Great. And an office on a main drag with your name in neon lights and a billboard or two around town advertising it," Bragg scowled. "But I wouldn't worry about it yet. Your name is last on the list. The first few names are guys in the Chicago area. Recognize anyone?"

"All of them," she said. They were dealers and runners she had met while posing as a supposed agent of The Barracuda. "What name are we down to?" she asked.

"The fourth, Lopez," Bragg said, pointing at it. "That means, if he stays consistent, there are four ahead of you in line."

A slow burn crept up Selena's neck. "Do you mean to tell me that you've waited until five hits before telling me I'm on this list?"

"Aw, don't get your shorts in a bundle," Bragg said. "Go easy, Selena. Have a heart — Father Johnny here had no idea it was a hit list at first, and by the time it was shown to us, we thought it looked like random drug hits or good ol' gangbanging. So it took a little while to connect the dots and then a little while longer to find you.

Like I said: your name is last. If he sticks to the order in the list, then we've got time."

"Question is: How much time?" She clapped the book shut. "When was the last one killed?"

"Thirteen days ago," Bragg said with military precision.

"Any timing pattern?"

"Not very consistent. We've got it plotted on a calendar. Twelve to fifteen days apart."

"So he's due," Selena noted. "What's your plan with these other guys, especially the next one on the list, Rodríguez? Is he under surveillance or are you going to pull him in for protective custody?"

"We'd use him for bait if we could find him," Bragg said with a shake of his head. "These guys are like roaches; you know that. They work hard at not being found. They don't exactly advertise their whereabouts. Some may have taken off, now that the fear of God has been put into them."

"He means it literally," Father Johnny said. "That's the other part you need to know."

Selena raised an eyebrow. "What part?"

"Shall I?" the cleric asked Bragg.

"Be my guest, Padre," Bragg said. "This is your territory."

"There is another tradition connected to the Day of the Dead I am sure you know," he began. "About the Aztec goddess *Mictecacihuatl*, also known as Lady Death."

"Oh, sure," Selena said with a little laugh and a flick of her wrist. "All Mexicans know her. The female grim reaper. When I was a kid, we decorated the house with paper-doll skeletons depicting her, and then my brothers and I got sugar skulls for presents."

"Candy skulls?" Bragg asked, making a face.

"With icing and sprinkles. I know, Del. It's not easy for *gringos* to understand. It's all lighthearted. Mexicans live with Lady Death easily and make fun of her. On the Day of the Dead, you're supposed to decorate your ancestors' graves with lots of flowers and have a major picnic in the cemetery with the whole family — aunts, cousins, everybody — and you take turns calling out insults to her like '*Ay, you old baldy, you missed me! I lived another year.*' "

"Let's hope she misses you this year," Bragg said.

"Some people think she is the one killing these men," Father Johnny said.

"You're not serious," Selena said.

"It gets better," Bragg said with a grin.

"Others," the priest went on, "say it is the Blessed Virgin of Guadalupe purifying her people and cleansing the community in advance of her great feast day on December 12."

Selena stared him in the eye. "I thought we all agreed that it's The Snake's enemies list."

The priest planted his palm on his chest, all sincerity. "When The Blue Lady makes her appearances —"

"Whoa, *un momentito*, hold it right there," Selena said. "What Blue Lady?"

"Haven't you heard about this in church?" Father Johnny asked with his forehead crinkled in surprise.

Selena pursed her lips. "I'm away most weekends," she said, "to visit my godmother and other *tías* and cousins in Chicago. I go to Mass with them there."

To make them happy, she thought. *But God and I aren't getting along, like my father and I never did. And from what I hear, God is stern like my own Papá, and I want nothing to do with him, and the Church too much like my critical Mamí.*

"No wonder I haven't seen you there," Father Johnny said, stoking her Catholic guilt. "Well, you are certainly most welcome at St. Mary's anytime. We are planning a most excellent celebration for the *Posada* and the Feast of Our Lady of Guadalupe."

She returned a noncommittal smile, the same one she used for informants asking for a better deal in court.

"I wouldn't if I were you, Selena," Bragg said. "If The Snake put the names in the book there, he might be on the lookout for you at St. Mary's."

The priest cocked his head, incredulous. "But your customers have not mentioned The Blue Lady either?"

"I stick to business," she said. But the truth was that she recalled a rumor to this effect in the public-library literacy program. She ignored it, a bit embarrassed by the religious hyperbole of poorly educated *Mexicanos*. Weren't the *supermercado* tabloids full of stories where people see the Virgin Mary on burnt toast, water stains under bridges, and misshapen potatoes?

The priest folded his hands and then eyed the ceiling, looking for the right words to begin. "Since August there has been — an *excitement* — over a little girl in Sterling Falls named Jacinta, an orphan who leaves her caretaker relatives often and visits area cemeteries to pray for the souls of the dead. She says a Blue Lady comes to her there and speaks to her, although sometimes the locutions, as they're called, come during the day, drawing a crowd of followers. The Blue Lady calls for prayer and repentance, and then announces judgment upon those who are victimizing her children and bringing shame upon her people. Most of my Latino parishioners believe it is Our Lady of Guadalupe, the patroness and protector of the Mexican people. Others say it is Lady Death herself."

"So what's the big deal? What does this have to do with The Snake?"

Bragg wagged the book. "Within forty-eight hours after this Blue Lady talks, one of these guys shows up dead."

"Have you questioned her? The girl, I mean?" Selena asked.

"She's hard to get hold of," Bragg said. "Every time we go to her home for questioning, she disappears."

Selena sprayed her fingers in midair. "Like — poof?"

"No," Bragg said. "There's a tight street network in that Hispanic neighborhood. People see white cops coming, the word spreads fast. And she's gone."

"Even outdoors," Father Johnny added, "she slips away because the crowds protect her as soon as they see *policias* coming."

"Another good reason to have you on board, Selena," Bragg said. "You'll fit right in. Maybe the girl will talk to a woman. Especially one who's brown like her."

"Maybe," Selena conceded, bristling a little at Bragg's habitual racism. "What else has she told others about this Blue Lady?"

"She says that The Blue Lady appears to her dressed in a blue cape decorated by yellow stars."

Bragg stifled a laugh.

"What's so funny?" Selena asked.

"It's rich. The Snake bumps off these guys and frames the Virgin Mary for it. He even leaves a serial-killer signature to make it stick."

"What signature?" Selena asked.

"Each time," the priest said, "the body has been found with flowers on it. Roses, marigolds, dahlias. That was the Blessed Mother's sign to Juan Diego at Guadalupe to prove to the bishop that she had appeared to him — flowers out of season tumbling from his *tilma*, with the miraculous image inside."

Selena knew the image well. All Mexicans did. *A woman clothed with the sun and the moon under her feet,* and this time looking much like an Aztec princess wrapped in royal turquoise. "Yes, I've seen it on display at the shrine in Mexico City," she said. "Our whole *familia* went on vacation there once."

The images tumbled back: *Mamí,* her *tías* and *Comadre* María and other female cousins approached the basilica on their bandaged knees, hands clasped in earnest prayer. But *Papá,* like any other indifferent *tourista* and believing that religion was for old women, took the three boys and Selena to the moving walkways to review the spectacular sight. Selena remembered how the Virgin Mother looked — humble, serene, and quiet. Nothing like her own mother shaking a mop at her and reproaching her about this-and-the-other small thing.

"So sad to think that any of our people would blame our Holy Mother for such things," the priest finished.

"So what do you make of The Blue Lady, Father?" Selena asked. "Is it a genuine apparition, or something else?"

"It's not for me to say," he said. "Only the Church, after a thorough investigation, can say. The diocese has only asked that I keep good records of the phenomenon for now. Then they might send a commission to look into the matter further. Suffice it to say that if it is genuine, then it is, like all of these manifestations, a *private* revelation and not a *public* one. Only Jacinta sees her, even in a public place with others around her. In all such similar cases, even those approved by the Church, the Virgin appears in a way the seer expects, filtered through the experience of that person. In this case, therefore, she looks like *La Virgen de Guadalupe*. That way, the seer recognizes her immediately."

"I'll tell you what it is," Bragg blustered. "It's gotta be The Snake dressed in some Halloween costume or *Day of the Dead* get-up jazzing this gullible little girl, using her to scare the crap out of his competition and hoping to throw us all off the track at the same time."

"It just doesn't sound like him," Selena said, puzzled. "He considers himself stylish but he's a drive-by killer. And leaving flowers? Can you trace them?"

"Colombia and Mexico," Bragg said with a nasal guffaw. "How's that for narrowing it down? A couple distributors in the region. Anyone can buy them in flower and garden shops, card and gift stores, a few dozen supermarkets, and hundreds of gas stations in the area — or online, for that matter. We tracked them down and got nothing."

"It's someone familiar with our customs, that's for sure," Selena noted. "Probably buying the flowers from a small Mexican market so it wouldn't appear to be unusual this time of year. Have you checked them out?"

Bragg pointed at her, pistol-style. "There you go. Another reason to bring you into the task force. These people will talk to you."

These people. These people who sneak across the border by the thousands. *These people* with large families who expect free health care. *These people* who take American jobs. *These people who* smuggle drugs and more of *these people. These people.* The racism ran just under the surface like the sewer pipe under the lawn. Bragg never seemed to care that *these people* lived in fear of discovery when they were only trying to earn money for their impoverished families back home, and many of *these people* died in the desert or in smugglers' locked trunks, or were stripped and held for ransom by their *coyote* guides once they arrived.

"It's more likely," she mused, "that they'll suspect me of undercover snooping for immigration. Where are the victims being killed, anyway?"

"In graveyards. Convenient, huh?"

"Where this girl has her visions?"

"Bingo."

"Do you suspect her?" Selena asked.

"She's just a girl, eleven or twelve," Bragg said. "She couldn't overpower these men. I'm tellin' ya, it's The Snake dressed as this 'Blue Lady' or working with a female accomplice who does the masquerade. We've been tracking this on a map. It's in the River Falls police station where we're setting up our operations center. You can get a full briefing there on the crime scenes and have a look at the photos and evidence. There's not much. Our offender cleans up real good. They're not finding anything except the flowers. And snake venom."

Selena leaned forward. "Venom?"

"Coroner says it's not the cause of death," Bragg said. "It would just take too much of the stuff. Our guess is that our bad guy, true to his name, uses a snake to surprise and stun them, giving himself the chance to slash them up at close quarters. That's what kills them, not the snake."

"I never knew The Snake kept a snake," Selena said.

"Makes sense," Bragg said. "He's a brand name now. Needs a trademark."

"There is an irony here, isn't there, with this talk of the snake and the Virgin?" Father Johnny said with his finger to his chin. "The Scripture says,

I will make you enemies of each other,
You, serpent, and the woman.
She will crush your head
And you will strike at her heels."

Bragg nodded toward Selena's slingbacks. "Like those?"

She stopped swinging her leg. "Very funny, Del. How come I haven't seen any of this in the papers?"

"You know us. We wanna keep it quiet. Why tip off the bad guys?"

Selena nodded. "Let's get back to the snake venom. What kind is it? Has a lab been able to identify the species?"

Bragg rolled his yes. "What a runaround. State Police sent it on to Illinois Wildlife Management, they sent it to the U of I, they sent it to the St. Louis Zoo herpetology people. We're still waiting."

"Did you check with area vets about anyone who keeps reptiles for pets or who have asked for advice or meds?"

"Yes," Bragg said. "Nothing there."

"How about pet stores?" Selena asked. "He might be buying mice or gerbils on a regular schedule. To feed the snake."

Bragg winced at the thought and said, "Did that. No dice."

Bragg's cell phone buzzed. He swore under his breath and excused himself to the kitchen.

Selena smoothed her wool Ann Taylor slacks and tapped her fingers on her knees nervously. The wall clock ticked. "Are you sure I can't interest you in some coffee, Father?" she asked. "Even if it isn't as fresh as you used to get in Panama?"

"How did you know that I was in the missions there?"

"Your accent," she said. "How about it?"

The priest held up a palm, almost in benediction. "No, thank you," he said. "You're very kind."

Bragg's grumbling echoed in the kitchen where a hinge squeaked and porcelain clinked. He was nosily inspecting her cabinets. Selena forced herself to stay seated.

Father Johnny shifted in his seat. "That must have been neat — your family vacation to Mexico City to see the shrine."

"Yes, it was."

"You say you see your family often?"

"Almost every weekend. In Chicago. My aunts, especially my godmother, María. My cousins. My two brothers. They visit me here. Sometimes." *When they're in trouble.*

"Your mother?"

"Gone. Heart condition."

"Your father?"

"He passed away the year after that visit to Mexico."

"I'm sorry."

I wasn't. Please don't make me talk about him.

"And you had another brother who passed away."

"Yes. A car accident in Germany, where he was an Army mechanic."

High on meth, Father. The performance drug. Makes you work harder, faster, more accurately and alertly, so you're feeling absolutely great for days without a hangover, except that after a while your brain is re-wired so that only meth can give you pleasure and nothing else, not food, not sex, and all real pleasure and any real emotion is denied you, leaving only fear and rage.

"And so you remember him and your mother every year in the Book of the Deceased."

"Yes."

"But not your father?"

She stopped tapping her fingers. *He came home late smelling of drink and another woman's perfume too often. He beat my Mamí when she challenged him. Once, when I tried to stop it, he threw me against the wall. It broke my left pinky finger, the one that is still a little crooked. That time, we told the doctor and my teachers I caught a soccer ball barehanded the wrong way.*

She took a breath. "Did I say I didn't?"

"No. Do you?"

Bragg strode in, snapping his phone shut. He remained standing. "We need to go," he announced. "River Falls police just located Rodríguez."

"That's the next man on the list," Father Johnny said.

"That's good," Selena said with a sigh of relief. She wouldn't have to say anything more about her family. "Let's go see what he knows."

"Too late," Bragg said. "He's dead."

CHAPTER 5

I don't do the killing myself. I like to watch. A blow to the victim's head, perhaps a little poison in their drink. That's all she wants me to do. Incapacitate them. Then I call her out.

She always looks beautiful when she's about to do it. Her curves ripple, her naked skin glistens, her dark pupils widen with — what shall I call it — joy. When her tongue wets her lower lip, the victim sometimes soils himself in fear, but the smell makes her more excited. She rises to her full height, flashes her perfect teeth and then strikes so fast I never really see it happen.

The fangs dig into the mouse's quivering back and walk toward the skinny tail, pulling the limp body deeper into her elastic throat.

Cihuacoatl, Heavenly Mother of the Aztecas, are you pleased? I have fed one of your divine children on Earth. Mihtoa Azteca: inech monequi. As the Aztec saying goes: it is necessary.

As it was last night.

CHAPTER 6

Selena directed Bragg to the mile-long straightaway of Sunrise Road outside of town, where he gunned the Chevy Tahoe's engine. The hulking SUV lunged like an angry bear, the speedometer needle arcing past 80 to 90. Father Johnny gulped and gripped the back seat, white-knuckled, but Selena absently gave her seat belt a reassuring tug. Bragg was showing off. Selena smirked to herself. Her Charger would leave him in the dust. She regularly burned carbon from her valves at 100 miles per hour in the first eighth of a mile on this very road — especially on those pre-dawn mornings when the recurring dreams startled her from sleep in a sweat. She'd go for 120 or more if she still had the chutes. Still, the adrenaline rush strangely calmed her, and it was starting to pump through her veins now.

Feed stores, body shops, the *Partes de Autos* junkyard and cows pressed against barbed wire zipped past in a blur; parked box cars on the Illinois Central tracks flashed by, *whoosh whoosh whoosh* — as familiar as flaggers at the Sinnissippi Dragway.

She'd always remember the day Antonio had taken her there to watch him race The Beast at the annual Power Wheel Standing Competition. The track manager had mistaken her for the new flag girl and shoved a zebra-striped umpire's shirt with black Lycra short-shorts into her gut and told her where to change and report. "*¡Insolente! ¡Descarado!*" she exploded. She snapped the short-shorts over the man's head, pulled them over his astonished face with a jerk, and stormed off.

"Did you have to do that?" Antonio steamed while driving out the gate, the manager glowering at him in the rearview mirror. "They said I can't race here anymore because of you."

"Go back," she said, thumping her chest with her thumb. "I'll drive. I'll show them what a *Latina* can do."

"You already did that," he said, gunning the gas to spin his back wheels. Gravel peppered the manager, and they both had laughed.

"So what d'ya know about this church cemetery we're going to?" Bragg called over the roar of the truck.

"Not much," Selena called back. "Old Presbyterian church dating from frontier days, where a Pentecostal Spanish-speaking church also meets. Is that right, Father?"

Father Johnny looked pale. He clearly never had the benefit of high-speed-chase training at the Academy. "Ye-yes," he stammered. "I met the pastor once. Clergy breakfast. Nice fellow. Does the work part-time."

"It'll be on that corner, Del," Selena said, recalling racing past its lonely parking-lot light. "Slow down."

Bragg floored the accelerator, and the Chevy leaped over a rise. He just averted a line of cars parked on the sandy shoulder.

"Who ARE all these people?" he complained. He pumped the brakes. Women and children milled about.

"Lots of visitors today," Selena said, eyeing the line of pickups and rusted beaters. A stream of people headed for the front gate.

Bragg screeched around the corner, braking hard. He craned his neck for a better look through a gathering crowd. The white steepled church was surrounded by the cemetery. The monuments converged on the little building, as though to insist on coming in. Yellow crime-scene tape fluttered along the high chain-link fence, starting above a worn sign, CEMETERY CLOSED SUNSET TO DAWN. VIO-LATORS SUBJECT TO ARREST. Coils of razor wire gleamed from the top. Selena knew why. It wasn't because of teenage vandals knocking over stones or spraying swastikas on them. It was meth dealers, coming to a central location among the many farms where ingredients to manufacture the poison was readily available.

Behind the entry gate, a County Sheriff's cruiser strobed its lights while two uniformed deputies stood watch, hat brims low, their mir-rored sunglasses working the crowd. When they saw Bragg pull up, they unlocked the chains with a clatter and swung one squealing gate open. Bragg chugged through, and the deputy shut the gate behind him with a clank.

The other deputy leaned to the opening driver-side window. "Agent Bragg," he acknowledged, inspecting the passengers. "Coroner's van just arrived. County crime-scene unit, too. Detective Gordon's been here a while."

"I'll take over from here," Bragg said. "Where's the command post?"

The officer pointed behind him. "Follow the yellow-brick road," he said, indicating a sandy set of ruts disappearing over a ridge. "There's an RV at the end of it. I'll announce you." He pressed a button on the crackling walkie-talkie attached to his shoulder and spoke sideways into it.

"This is your stop, Padre," Bragg said over his shoulder. "No need to crowd the crime scene."

"I'll ask if anyone saw something," he said, getting out.

"Let us do the interviewing," Bragg said.

Selena turned to him, imploring with her hands. "Del, they might be more open to a Spanish-speaking priest instead of an Anglo —"

"Let us do the police work," Bragg snapped. "Tell everyone you're here for last rites or whatever Catholics call it, but we won't let you until we're done processing the crime scene, OK? See ya, Padre." He waited. The priest nodded gently and briefly smiled at Selena before getting out. The door shut. Bragg punched the gas.

"That wasn't necessary," Selena huffed. "They have no reason to fear him."

"They got no reason to fear me, either, if they're legal and don't have anything funny in their pockets."

Selena twisted to study the growing tangle of people outside the gate. A cinnamon-skinned mother in a shawl and her young teenage daughter shouldered through a circle of bystanders to lay a bouquet of flowers beside a rising mound of garlands, wreaths, candles, and prayer cards against the chain-link fencing. Men and women clustered around the newcomers and began to thumb rosaries, heads bowed. Selena lost sight of them when the SUV dipped sharply over the ridge past gnarly burr oaks down to a pond.

This was a yet-to-be-filled area, not as well-tended as the rest. The grounds looked sandy, crisscrossed by gravel pathways wide enough for a hearse. A line of officers conducted a grid search. All the trees had been cleared, the trunks ground up to kill them completely and prevent their thirsty roots from ruining the graves yet to be dug and the mothers, fathers, brothers, and neighbors yet to fill them. Illinois required concrete vaults to protect coffins and urns, but over decades, a tree's roots found a way to claim a buried body.

Clusters of ash and honey locusts pressed at the fence like box-seat fans at Wrigley Field. A row of white pines whispered behind them, and Selena wondered what they were saying about what happened last night in the serene lagoon, now surrounded by orange cones marking the perimeter of the crime scene.

The SUV's wheels ground on the newly frozen dirt, crunching like corn flakes. A black-and-white cruiser, the coroner's van and county crime-scene truck were parked well away from the water, lined up behind an RV serving as the command post. A pathway angling down to the water's edge marked with yellow tape indicated the cleared entry access, to prevent contamination of the scene.

A uniformed officer with a clipboard under his armpit stepped from the RV.

Bragg crunched to a stop and got out. "You the first officer?" he asked.

"Yes, sir. Lundgren, sir," the officer replied. He nearly saluted. He flipped his clipboard to record their names and the arrival time. Champion of the police clipboard drill team, Selena thought as she slammed the door.

"Tell me what we've got, Lundgren," Bragg ordered.

"Male Hispanic, 25 to 30 years of age, dead on the scene," Lundgren reported flatly. "Cuts on the neck and a single stab wound just below the ribcage."

"I'll ask the coroner for the details. No suspect in custody, I understand?"

"Correct, sir."

"Witnesses?"

"No, sir. One of the church elders did a routine walk-around first thing in the morning, checking for vandalism, beer cans, and what-not, and saw the body in the water. He's in the RV here and pretty shook up. Name is Lopez. Want me to get his statement? He speaks English."

"I'll do that," Bragg said.

"It looks like the man made a few more calls besides calling 911. You probably saw all the people as you drove in."

"Be sure to keep them out," Bragg said. "There's too many people here as it is. We'll try to interview some of them. Maybe someone saw something, or our offender has returned to check out the scene. Come on, Selena, let's go find Detective Gordon."

They made their way down the slope to the grotto. At the twenty-five-yard perimeter, yellow crime-scene tape fluttered and announced in two languages: CRIME SCENE — DO NOT CROSS/SCENA DE CRIMEN — NO CRUZAR. They put on latex gloves from a cardboard box and pulled blue shoe covers from a dispenser. Selena was glad she'd changed into her cobalt-blue Roxy Lulu ballet flats.

Technicians swarmed over the scene like ants on a mound, snapping photos, drawing sketches, laying out yellow tape measures and dropping little numbered tents to indicate bits of evidence. The coroner and her assistant knelt by a body that was sprawled face down in the water. The pond's edges had frozen to shimmering cellophane over the cold November night, and it looked as though the half-submerged man had fallen through a pane of glass. Blood pooled beneath him, fanning out like the petals of a black rose. Marigolds floated in the water, twirling slowly like ballerinas. Dahlias danced beside them.

A stocky man in a dun raincoat standing by a white concrete bench and plain wooden cross, a spot for quiet contemplation, noticed the new arrivals. He gave an instruction to a photographer beside him and then strode toward Bragg and Selena, his arms swinging like sledgehammers.

"Agent Bragg," Detective Frank Gordon of the River Falls Police Department acknowledged, "and Miss De La Cruz. How the devil are ya? Golly, ex-DEA, huh? You sure had us fooled."

"That was the point," Selena said.

"From undercover agent to insurance agent, huh? Quite a jump, isn't it?"

"Both jobs are about assessing risk," she countered, "and good at thinking ahead about what might go wrong."

"Sure." Gordon turned to Bragg and jerked his thumb at Selena. "So what's she doing here?"

Selena tightened her stomach.

"She's part of the team," Bragg said. "Isn't that right, Selena?"

"I —"

"I thought she was gonna lay low," Gordon interjected. "Go to Chicago, even. Stay with her family or a safe house."

"I'm on the *list*," Selena said with an emphatic wave of her hand.

"Exactly," Gordon said. "You'll be too emotionally involved to be much good to —"

"Too emotionally involved?" Selena cut him off, regretting the raised voice. She took it down a notch. "That's the best reason —"

"The best reason to butt out and stay under the radar. You've proven that you're already good at that."

Bragg stepped up to Gordon, chest to chest. "I'm in charge here, and she's on the case."

Every hair of Gordon's crewcut stood up. "This is a homicide, not a drug bust, and hence under my jurisdiction."

Bragg leaned forward, nose to nose. "This guy is on our list of dealers and was probably lured here by the promise of a big deal."

"Let's get this straight," Gordon said. "Until we get a positive ID on this guy or find evidence of drugs, this is a local matter and I'm the one in charge."

"I was told on the phone that he had a wallet with an ID and five thousand dollars still in it," Bragg said. "What more do you want?"

"Oh, gee, I don't know," Gordon said, his rolling eyes searching the slate-gray sky, "fingerprint confirmation, maybe? Coroner Gates is getting impressions with the lab guy now. Blood and tissue samples are already on the way to the state DNA lab. A wallet can be planted, huh? Just maybe? Leave this to our homicide division. When we need some doors busted in, we'll call you."

Bragg harrumphed in the condescending way he did with street punks and called to the woman crouched beside the partly submerged corpse. "Coroner Gates?"

"That's me," said the woman with cheeks pinked from the cold. "Pleased to meetcha." A wool ski cap covered the tips of her ears, where a surgical mask was attached. She snapped shut a plastic container for the fingertip impressions to be studied later.

"Can you estimate a time of death yet?" Bragg asked.

"Within twenty-four hours, for sure," Gates replied. "I'd even guess early last evening, near 6 p.m., judging by the purple lividity. I put a thermometer in the chest cavity but the cold temperatures overnight might throw off the calculation. Being half in the water didn't help, but it was too cold overnight for much bloating or fatty adipocere to form."

"I thought so," Bragg said. He snapped his gloves in Gordon's face, leaned down to the water, reached in front of the startled woman and gripped the head of the dead man by the stiff black hair. He yanked the face out of the water with a sucking sound. He twisted the head sideways. "Hey, Selena — is this Rodríguez?"

She could tell in a moment — that frozen, snaggletooth leer, the eyes blank as they had been in life, the pencil-thin mustache he'd always tugged at nervously as though to help it grow. A dark line crossed the throat.

"It's him," Selena confirmed, a tide of nausea rising in her belly.

Bragg dropped the limp head back into the water with a *splish*. "Well, there's your positive ID, Gordon. And a good reason to have Selena on the team and not stashed away in protective custody. Get it?"

Gordon jammed his fists into his coat pockets. To keep from punching Bragg, Selena thought. *You're not the only one ever tempted to do it, amigo.* Like that time on the Academy shooting range when he shoved his knee between her thighs from behind and kicked her feet apart. *Ya gotta spread 'em and squat, honey. Like you're sitting on a barstool. Dominant-side foot back a little. Good, just like that.* Then he smacked her fanny once and moved on.

Bragg spanked water from his gloves. "So what's your working theory, Gordon? Besides the fact that our guy lured him out here for a promising deal and popped him, leaving the money behind and his flowers. Is this the murder scene or a dump site?"

"We're not sure yet. Sir." Gordon said it between his teeth.

"Is there another escape route besides the front gate? Any digging under the chain-link fencing back there?"

"Yes, one spot but it's too small for a man to shimmy through. We're looking for tire impressions and shoe prints but the frozen ground isn't helping. I've got patrol officers at Rodríguez's residence looking over his car."

"There's something about the fingerprints you'll want to know," piped up the coroner, closing a leather case and standing up. "When I took the prints, I found bite marks on the right hand."

"Snake bite, right?" Bragg said.

"Four clean punctures," Coroner Gates affirmed. "We'll check the venom in the autopsy. Snakes detect prey by smell, you know, especially sweat and an excess of carbon dioxide. In other words, they're attracted to fear. Our killer probably used a snake to intimidate the victim but it's probably not what killed him. Rarely enough venom for that."

"Stabbing, the first officer tells me," Bragg said.

"Slit throat, and one thrust below the rib cage to the heart," the coroner surmised.

"He's getting more efficient," Bragg said.

"Practice makes perfect, huh?" Gordon said darkly.

"Funny thing is," Gates added, "there's no tear in his shirt. The jacket is unzipped and the shirt tugged out of his belt."

"So he was a sloppy dresser," Bragg said. "They all are."

"But it was a cold night," Selena said. "He'd have his jacket zipped. So our guy stabbed him in the belly after the fact, just to be sure he was dead?"

Coroner Gates shrugged. "I'll know more after the autopsy."

A technician called Gordon away. Bragg leaned close to Selena. "So what is it?" Bragg asked under his breath. "Are you in or not?"

Selena swallowed hard. "I'm in," she said. "Only as a consultant, mind you. Temporary."

"C'mon, you miss this. You're an adrenaline junkie."

"I'm not re-enlisting, Del. Understand?"

Bragg grinned in triumph. "Sure. I don't want you to quit the insurance day job. It's a good cover. But you'll need to get away from it more often. Find a good excuse. And tell the guy you've been seeing, Rick —"

"Reed."

"Whatever. Tell him you can't see him for a while. He'll just get in the way, you know."

"We've got a date this Saturday."

"Call it off."

"I can't do that."

"Sure you can. You get on the phone and cancel."

"I won't do that."

"Afraid you'll lose this one like the others?" Bragg said.

She pressed her hand to her side to keep from slapping him. "This one's different. He's not a cop."

"Whatever. But he'll find out soon enough you're as high maintenance as your car."

"I'm keeping the date," she said.

"Fine. Just be sure to give him the big brush-off then," Bragg urged.

"I'll have to tell him why."

"Tell him nothing. You hear me? Nothing. You tell him you're too busy to see him for a while, or you dump him outright. Tell him he's not your type. He isn't, right? An egghead professor and a little old for you, from what I hear."

"He's funny. He's smart." *He is a caballero,* a gentleman and *muy* handsome. *Mamí would have liked him.*

"He's history. Do whatever it takes. Get it?"

Selena's heart squeezed. Did it have to be this way every time? Who could ever stay together in this work?

"Did you hear me?" Bragg said. His voice softened. "Look, Selena — you know how these guys operate. They get to you by getting to your loved ones first if they can."

She bit her lower lip. "I hear you."

"Glad you see it my way," Bragg said, reaching into his jacket. "Here's a badge."

Selena snatched the palm-size leather case with the gold DEA shield and slid it into her coat pocket.

"And here's your piece," he added, drawing a pistol from his belt holster. "It's unloaded."

He yanked back the slide on the gun with a sharp ca-click and handed it open-action to her sideways, barrel pointed to an empty area.

"I've already taken care of the FOID card," Bragg continued, producing two magazines loaded with 9-millimeter cartridges. "You might want to get a little practice on a range sometime. Work on that stance of yours."

Selena hefted the P226 Sig Sauer semiautomatic, slammed the slide back in place and checked the decocker. Agents described it as a "friendly" gun, with an easy trigger — too easy for some. The smaller model molded to her hand. It felt warm, and heavier than she remembered. She tested its balance, finger extended alongside the locator above the trigger. It smelled faintly of fresh oil. Funny how she'd always wanted a real gun ever since those drenching water-pistol fights with her brothers on the Feast of Saint John the Baptist. She took the oversize magazines. Fifteen 9 mm rounds each.

"Don't spend them all in one place," Bragg said. "And you'd better load it and go hot right away. Start by talking to those people at the gate. Mingle and ask questions. Maybe somebody saw something. Don't say you're with us. Just be the insurance agent you are."

"Some of them will wonder why I drove in with the police," she said, shoving one of the magazines into the handle with a fluid push and a satisfying snap.

"That's easy," Bragg said. "Tell them you just needed a positive ID to pay out Mr. Rodríguez's life insurance."

Angry shouts drifted over the ridge. The splinter of breaking glass. A shotgun boom.

Ay Dios mio, Selena whispered. She rammed the pistol in her belt, pocketed the spare magazine, and sprinted to the entry.

CHAPTER 7

Father Johnny was waiting for her, grasping the chain-link fence, worry creasing his face. Behind him, an uneasy throng of people milled about. They murmured like angry bees. Men punched fists into the air; women wept on each other's shoulders. When another squad car screeched up, the crowd gathered and shouted at the officers.

You have no right!

¡Ustedes no entienden!

The officers lined up shoulder to shoulder and fixed their fists on their batons.

"Father, what happened?" Selena called.

"They took her," Father Johnny answered over the catcalls.

"Took who? What's going on?"

"That young girl we saw on the way in. It's Jacinta. The visionary. The police took her."

"Where?"

"To the station."

"They arrested her?"

"No. For questioning. I tried to stop them, but they said she is a possible witness to a crime and they have the right to take her."

Rocks pelted the cruisers. Some men whistled. The officers drew their nightsticks, and the one with the shotgun cocked it menacingly for another warning shot.

Selena tore off the crime-scene shoe covers and pushed past the *padre*. "Help me calm these people down, Father," she said.

She weaved through some bystanders and pulled her badge from her jacket. She flashed it at the officers, close to her chest so the crowd wouldn't see it. The officers nodded.

"Hey, we finally got her," one said.

"Look at this crowd," Selena scolded. "You got more than you bargained for." She pocketed the badge wallet quickly, brushed past the startled officers and vaulted onto the dented hood of the cruiser. She raised her arms.

"*¡Escúchenme, señores y señoras, por favor! Listen to me!*"

The rock-throwing halted.

"Please," she continued in Spanish, "let's be calm. Does it please Our Lady, Queen of Peace, if we act in such a manner?"

"The *policías gringos* arrested her for no reason!" someone called. "It is an *insulto* and an offense to Our Lady, who speaks to her!"

The crowd assented with calls.

Selena waved her arms to regain attention. "Our Lady can uphold her own *honor, mis compadres*. And the girl was not arrested, just taken in for questions. No harm will come to her. I will see to it."

"So you work for the *policía* now?" a man called.

She stuck out her palms, imploring. "*Amigos*, you know me. I'm one of you. Some of you are my customers, *sí*? Like you, Paulo. I just sent you a bill with that special discount. Didn't you get it?"

"No," the man replied.

"Look for it. And listen: the police are taking me in for questioning too."

"*¡Híjole!*"

"*¿Por qué?*"

"How dare they!"

"It's not that. I have insurance information about the man who was killed in there. They need it for their investigation. But while I am there, I will see Jacinta and make sure she is all right. I promise. Meanwhile, you must stay calm, and remain in prayer. Isn't that what she would ask you to do?"

Shoes shuffled. Hands plunged into pockets. Women whispered and nodded.

Father Johnny stepped forward and faced the assembly. "*Hermanos y hermanas*, brothers and sisters, let us join our hearts before our Lord and ask Our Lady of Guadalupe for her prayers and protection. In the name of the Father and of the Son and of the Holy Spirit —"

Heads bowed.

"¡*Madre amorosa, María Santísima de Guadalupe!*" Father Johnny intoned. "*Bien lo sabéis Señora, bien sabéis que desde mi tierna edad, os he mirado y reverenciado como Madre, como abogada y protectora —*"

Selena dismounted the squad car while Father Johnny invoked the Virgin Mother. The officers tugged off their glasses and glanced from Selena to the dented hood.

"Relax, fellas," she said, "it was banged up already. And you've got good auto insurance — don't you?"

Detective Gordon passed by in his unmarked Impala as Bragg pulled up in the Tahoe and beckoned her in.

"They need you at the station," he said. "Get in." He sped away once Selena had snapped her seat belt. "The girl's English isn't good."

"I expected that."

"Hey, it looked like you were giving a little speech. What'd you say to settle down the crowd?"

"I told them I had a special this week on term-life-insurance policies. Like the guy in the pond, you never know when you'll need it."

CHAPTER 8

A uniformed officer arose from his cluttered desk and half-finished pizza slice to greet them. He rubbed his hands on a napkin and grinned. "Hey, Miss De La Cruz, how are you —"

"Where is she, Officer Reardon?" Selena demanded.

His face fell. This wasn't a casual meeting at a fender-bender scene. "Gee, you can't —"

"It's all right," Gordon said from behind her, "I asked her to come. She'll help us talk to the girl."

"Interview Room One," Reardon said, a wad of dough stuck in his cheek.

"I'll handle this with Selena," Bragg said, striding toward the door.

"This is my station," Gordon objected.

"We already had this conversation," Bragg replied. "This is my case, remember? C'mon, Selena."

Gordon firmed his lips. "I'll be in observation."

"How is she?" Selena asked Reardon over her shoulder.

"Real quiet. Scared, I guess."

"Anyone with her?"

"No."

"You left a little girl alone in that room?"

"Standard procedure, ma'am."

Selena tapped her temple with her fingers, thinking *Ay, que menso*. She joined Bragg and Gordon in a corridor past a safety-glass door. It shut behind her, muffling the scanner-radio chatter and ringing phones.

Gordon stepped into the next room down, where the recording equipment was.

Selena smoothed her hair back. "Let me do this alone, Del. She'll be frightened —"

"That's not a bad thing," he said, opening the door for her.

She stepped inside. The girl looked up from doodling on photocopy paper with a colored pencil.

"Jacinta?" Selena said with a gentle smile, lowering herself into the metal chair opposite the table and looking the girl in the eyes.

They were soft tan, the hue of a newborn fawn, not the Indian black Selena had expected. Jacinta shyly brushed away a chocolate-colored bang that fell across her line of sight, and it stuck in place. The oily hair hadn't been washed in a long time. Two braids, bound by elastic bands, framed the sallow cheeks.

"*Usted no es mi tía,*" the girl said.

"No, I am not your aunt," Selena replied in Spanish, then to Bragg, shouldered against the wall behind her: "She was expecting a relative."

"She was pulled in as a witness and maybe even a suspect," Bragg said. "I'm sure they're trying to track down someone from her family. Remember, her mother's dead and her father's deported. We think there's an aunt or a cousin around."

That explained the girl's comment. "*Mi nombre es Selena,*" Selena said to identify herself, smiling at the girl.

"Are you a *mujer policía?*" Jacinta asked.

"No, I'm not a police woman," Selena replied in Spanish. "A business woman. I sell insurance. I work with the police when there is a car accident or a house fire. Sometimes the police ask me to translate for them."

"You're very pretty," the girl said.

"So are you," Selena said. The girl's voice sounded dry and brittle. "*¿Tienes sed, Jacinta?* Would you like some water?"

"*Agua, sí.*"

"When was the last time you had something to eat, *pequeña hija?*" Little daughter. Her own mother and godmother called her that. Jacinta shrugged. "*Ayer por la mañana.*"

"Yesterday morning? Good heavens, Del, they didn't offer her anything to eat."

"This is a police station, not a cafeteria."

"Get something now."

Bragg pointed brusquely at the mirror on the wall to Gordon behind it.

"You will have something in a moment, Jacinta," she assured the girl. "Have they been kind to you in other ways?"

"They let me use the bathroom," she said. "They gave me some soap to wash with."

There was still a ripe dumpster smell about her. It clung to the threadbare sweater with the worn-through elbows, the too-small jeans. "Do you know why you are here?" Selena asked quietly.

"*Sí*," Jacinta said, "to ask me questions, but I cannot answer any of them."

"Why not?"

"I do not know what they are asking. I think they want me to say something about the man in the cemetery. But I did not see anything. I only saw The Blue Lady. And The Blue Lady said not to speak with those who will not believe."

Is that the real reason for her silence? Selena wondered.

"Do you believe in her?" Jacinta asked.

Believe in whom? Selena wondered. The Blue Lady? Mary? To Jacinta, they were the same, according to Father Johnny. To Selena, this was still a mystery to be resolved.

"Do you?" Jacinta repeated.

"When I was a young *niña*, like you," Selena said, "I kept all her feast days, especially *la Fiesta de Nuestra Señora de Guadalupe*. I loved how the *Maríachis* played at Mass." It wasn't a lie. It was a cultural thing.

"I will tell her," Jacinta said, a smile breaking across her weary face.

"What did she tell you?" Selena asked.

"She said someone bad was going to die. She was sad. Her Son is very angry, she said, and punishments must come to the ones who harm his people."

Even God had a good-cop, bad-cop thing going, Selena thought. The angry Son and the gentle Mother staying his hand. Selena asked gently, "Did she tell you the name of the man who was going to be punished?"

"No."

"Did she say where or when the punishment would happen?"

"No."

"Did she describe how it would happen?"

"No."

"Did she say anything else?"

"Only that her people must return to her and pray and this would please her Son."

"And where did she speak to you?"

"In a little cemetery, far out in the fields. Where I pray for the dead. It has old white stones and the names almost gone."

So it wasn't in that Presbyterian/Pentecostal cemetery after all. She hadn't seen anything. Might there be some evidence in the little cemetery Jacinta had been in? The Illinois countryside was dotted with such plots, memorials to local Civil War dead. Selena made a mental note to contact the Illinois Cemetery Commission for a map of every graveyard in the county.

"Does she always speak to you there?"

"Different places."

"Can you show us where this place was?"

She hesitated. "I think so. I do not think she will be angry if I do."

"When did she speak to you there?"

"Two days ago. In the night. It was very dark. There was no moon."

"Jacinta, was there anyone else there with you?"

"Not this time. Some other times, when I am home, sí. Many follow me when I know she is calling to me."

"How do you know she is calling?"

"I just know. I hear her in my head."

"How long were you with the Lady this time, Jacinta?"

"I don't know. Time means nothing when I am with her," the girl said, wistful.

"Did you hear anything else, Jacinta?"

"I only heard the Lady speak."

"In Spanish, of course."

Jacinta laughed. A girlish giggle, so innocent. Selena noted the grass stains on her jeans' knees, from a soccer-game fall — or from her praying. "*Español, por supuesto. ¿Así hablan en el cielo, no?*"

"Yes, Spanish is the language of heaven," Selena agreed.

Bragg bit at one of his nails. "Ask her what the lady looks like," he said.

"All right," Selena said. "Jacinta, tell me more about *La Señora Azul*. What does she look like?"

The girl brightened as though the slate of the November sky had split and the sun was piercing it for the first time in days. "Like this," she said, pulling a sheet of paper from the little pile on the table. She held up a colored-pencil drawing of a woman in a cloak.

"*Es mi madrecita,*" Jacinta swooned.

"Is that her?" Bragg asked. "Our primary suspect?"

Selena ignored him and studied the sketch of a serene woman dressed in a white gown with an ankle-length blue veil spangled with yellow stars. Her jet-black hair parted just off-center and flowed behind the veil. The dark eyes were half-closed and demurely downcast toward hands folded in prayer at the chest, just above the black bow of a cloth belt. Jacinta had colored the hands and face cerulean blue. It was, without question, Our Lady of Guadalupe appearing as a pregnant Aztec princess to the Indian Juan Diego at Tepeyac Hill, whose image on the peasant's cloak convinced the skeptical local bishop and nine million Aztec converts in 1541. Like all Mexicans, Jacinta would have seen the image thousands of times. The girl was a good artist. Selena could hardly draw stick figures.

"*¡Ay, ella es hermosa!*" the girl said dreamily. "Her hair is so black, it is blue, do you know what I mean? And her veil, it is the blue like my aunt's turquoise ring, and it makes a glow so that everything around her shines blue as well, even her face, so filled with peace. Here are the golden stars on the veil, all the way down to her feet. It is not such a fine picture, but you may have it, *Señorita* Selena," Jacinta offered.

"*Gracias*, Jacinta. It is very kind of you. It is a very good picture." Bragg would have kept it as evidence anyway.

A rap sounded at the door, and Gordon entered, balancing a tray loaded with clinking glasses of ice water and a submarine sandwich in wax paper.

"Hey, that looks like the ham-and-cheese sub I put in the fridge for dinner," Bragg said.

"It is," the detective said.

Gordon placed the tray in front of Jacinta, and she drained the glass nearest to her, looking up over the rim with those large fawn eyes. Selena had seen eyes like that before, wide in fright, aiming at her in the shadows — or so she thought — before Selena squeezed off two shots in self-defense. The girl's scream still awakened her at night.

Jacinta put the emptied glass down. The ice cubes rattled. She folded her hands in her lap.

"Aren't you hungry?" Selena asked.

The girl nodded, and the braids swung playfully. "I am, but my stomach, it hurts."

Not from hunger, Selena surmised. The girl was traumatized, pulled into this starkly lit, hospital-green cinderblock room by men in uniforms with guns who didn't speak her language and then left her by herself.

Officer Reardon poked in.

"We made contact with the aunt," he announced. "She was already on the way. She'll be here any minute. Name is Eva Sandoval."

"*Encontramos a tus tía Eva, Jacinta*," Selena informed her. "You can leave soon."

"*Por favor, se lo ruego*, do not send me away with her," Jacinta pleaded. She seized Selena's hand. "Do not let her take me. You must not."

The girl's terror electrified her.

"Why not, little daughter?" Selena asked.

"She will beat me," Jacinta cried. "She does not believe. She and my uncles and cousins say I am sick. I am not sick. I have seen Our Lady. She speaks to me, and I cannot help it."

Selena turned to Bragg. "She's afraid of her. She abuses her. No wonder she runs away. Can't you do anything?"

"DCFS thing," he huffed. "Not my issue."

"Detective Gordon?"

"Sorry. There's no evidence of abuse to act on."

"Keep her here, then," Selena said.

Bragg pushed air through his nose, a scoff. "We can't detain her. She's a minor. She's not under arrest. And if someone from her family claims her, she's gotta go."

Selena turned to the girl who was wiping away a silver tear from her eye with her sleeve.

"I'm sorry, little daughter," Selena said, "but we must send you home with your *familia*."

Jacinta sniffled. "Can I not go home with you, *Señorita* Selena? You would keep me safe, no?"

A lump rose in Selena's throat. Her eyes misted.

Bragg noticed. "What's the matter? What'd she say?"

"She wants to go home with me," Selena said, her breath still caught short.

Jacinta suddenly leaped from the chair and embraced Selena. The girl's warmth washed through Selena's body like a summer breaker on the beach at Acapulco. The girl's tears burned on her neck.

"Can we go now, please?" the girl pleaded. "I'm afraid."

"Taking her home," Gordon said, "would be, legally speaking, kidnaping. You can't do it, Miss De La Cruz. We deal with these DCFS people all the time. We'd all be written up, suspended, and hauled into court."

"I know that," Selena said, stroking Jacinta's hair. It was slick and tangled, in need of a good brushing. She hugged the girl closer and said in her ear, "Do not be afraid, little one. I will come to visit you, to be sure you are well. I promise."

The corridor door swung open, admitting shouts from the squad room.

"Lady, take it easy —"

"*¿Donda esta mi sobrima?* Where is that little *mocosa*? Bring her to me now! *¡Pronto!*"

The girl shuddered.

"That must be them," Reardon said, dismissing himself. The door clicked shut, cutting off the raised voices.

Selena gripped the girl's shoulders. "I will see you again, little daughter," she promised again.

Jacinta buried her face in Selena's blouse.

"They will beat me," she whimpered.

CHAPTER 9

Selena led Jacinta into the squad room by the hand, the little girl's grip on her tightening with each step.

"*There* you are," scolded a puffy-cheeked woman in a pink parka. Her dark hair, streaked with bottled highlights, was pulled back in a bun and a dragon tattoo growled at her neckline. "Get over here! *¡Eres una vergüenza!* Shame!"

Two men in leather jackets, ostrich cowboy boots, and Western hats stood behind her. Their eyes darted around like nervous sparrows.

Officer Reardon produced a clipboard with a form. "Miss Sandoval, I need your signature to release the girl. Right here."

The glaring woman dashed it off and thrust the pen back at him. She lunged and locked onto Jacinta by the forearm.

Selena held on.

"*Suéltala,*" Eva Sandoval spat. "You will let her go."

"We need her," Selena said through her teeth, "to help us find whoever is killing all those men, like the one in the cemetery today."

"Whoever it is, he can keep on killing them," she sneered. "They are trash! *¡Parásitos!* They deserve to die. Now let go, I tell you!"

Jacinta whined from the painful pressure of her aunt's grip, turning the girl's thin arm white. Selena released her. Jacinta cried out as the woman tore her away.

Eva shook a finger in Selena's face. "You have a lot of nerve."

"I do," Selena said, "and if any harm comes to the girl you will answer to me."

"You stay away from her, and from us," the woman said, dragging Jacinta away. "And what lies have you been telling the *policía,* eh?"

"*La Señora Azul* —" Jacinta began.

"*Estoy harta*, enough with this Blue Lady nonsense," Eva scolded in her ear. She eyed Selena. "Whatever she told you, do not believe it. She is very sick, and a liar." She spun on her heel, called *¡Vamos!* to the men, and stormed out. At the door, she gave Selena an over-the-shoulder leer of victory. Jacinta twisted around for a last teary-eyed glance before being yanked outside.

Once the door had slammed, Selena ran her fingers through her hair. She sighed deeply. "That went well, don't you think?"

"Forget it, Selena," Bragg said. "Let's debrief and review the case board so you're up to speed."

"Forget it, Del," she returned. "I'm beat. I'm going home. I need a big Margarita and a good night's sleep. I can come in the morning after my client appointments, say, around 11."

"The longer you wait, the closer he gets," Bragg warned.

"Good, that's what I'm hoping for," she said, her fingers curled up and gesturing *bring it on*.

CHAPTER 10

It always starts with the drive-by surveillance, a tactical recon in an unmarked van by the B-Team, looking for fortifications and lookouts.

"Basement windows are all painted black, and there's a cable goin' up to the attic," the radio squawks, "so it's finished off up there. No fire escape. Garage out back to run into. Uh-oh. Dog run. Yup. Pit bull. Mean lookin', too."

"We're gonna have to neutralize him right away," Bragg says into the walkie-talkie.

"Quiet otherwise. No bad guys on the porch or anywhere."

"All right, Montana One, you take the outbuilding as planned and we'll deploy to the north entry of the house."

"Copy that."

Bragg sips his Wendy's Big Slurper. "Ladies, let's brief on this one more time."

Seven men cluster closely around him and Selena finds herself shouldered outside the circle.

"The suspect is a mid-level dealer, and he might have a bodyguard or two," Bragg warns them. "We'll use a flash-bang and split in two when we get inside. It looks like there's a finished attic, so the stairway up to it might be closed, a fatal funnel. So watch out. DJ, you carry in another ram in case there's a door at the top. B-team will cover the perimeter with two guys in APR masks and Nomex suits."

"There's no meth lab," Selena pipes up from the back. "You won't need the respirators. I told you it's just a boy selling his mother's pain pills from the back porch."

"The basement windows are painted over," Bragg shoots back. "There's something down there they want to hide. Even if it's just stolen property, I want a rescue team ready if it's a meth lab down there and the place blows from a spark."

"Then why use the grenades?"

"It's better than ringing the doorbell," Bragg says, and the men laugh. "OK, let's dress out and get this show on the road."

Seated in the van, Selena tightens the helmet's chin strap over the black face mask. The men press on helmets and hug their semiautomatics fitted with lights and lasers; she has a flashlight and the 9 mm Sig Sauer. She pats the dagger in an ankle sheath she's worn ever since that close call in Cuernavaca.

"Count down for me, DJ," Bragg calls from the driver's seat.

DJ calls out the numbers remaining to the target house, beginning ten houses away. They zip by in a blur. TenNineEightSeven. It's a way to avoid going to the wrong house — like last time.

SixFiveFour.

The adrenaline rush kicks in. The van door is thrown open like a plane hatch before the paratroopers launch. The chilly morning air howls in Selena's helmet.

ThreeTwo.

ONE.

"Go, go!" Bragg barks, the van still rolling to a stop.

They leap out, hit the ground running, knees flexed, weapons up, moving, moving, moving in a snaking single file to the entrance. The ram swings into the door once. Twice. It splinters open.

"Police! Search warrant!"

The grenade detonates inside, a jolting thump, and the men charge through the thin white smoke. A dog barks outside. A pistol fires. *Pop pop.* There is no more barking.

"Down! Get down! Show me your hands!" an officer shouts. A dazed boy on the living-room couch drops to the floor. An officer strips off the sheet he was sleeping in and wrenches the boy's arm behind him. The boy yelps.

Selena draws the Sig Sauer and races up the stairs, last in the line, boots thundering on the steps ahead of her.

"Outbuilding is secure," a walkie-talkie crackles.

The men burst into the first bedroom, crouching, flashing their lights into every corner. Girlie room. Lace, ruffles. A dresser with perfumes and a TV. The bed is rumpled but empty. The men file out to check the next room. Selena feels the TV; it's warm. She spies the pillow on the floor, the bedspread corner pulled too far down, pointing to the closet. She yanks open the door, ducks back into a squat, pistol raised.

The shadow inside aims at her.

Selena fires.

The girl wails in pain. Slumps forward. Her pigtails droop. She drops the TV remote control.

It spins at Selena's feet.

"You did it again," Bragg cackles from behind her.

She turns. He grins. She empties the rest of the ammo magazine into him *bambambambambam.*

She wakes up.

She weeps.

CHAPTER 11

In the morning, after servicing two policy changes and one auto accident, Selena excused herself from the office. She knew she ought to stay in this slow season of the year, building her book of business with a holiday mailing and expiration-date phone calls.

"Hold my calls except for an *emergencia*," she told Felicia, handing her a card. "And when this independent adjuster shows up, send him to this address."

"I will," the receptionist replied, not looking up from her paperwork.

"I'll be out for the rest of the day." Selena leaned over, angled her chin, and squinted. "That's quite a bruise you have, *mija*."

Felicia feathered her bangs, covering an olive mark veined with purple. Her cheeks pinked. "I — I fell."

"You don't lie very well," Selena said. "It's that boyfriend of yours, what's his name —"

"Marco."

"He hit you again?"

"It was an accident."

Selena shook her head. "Listen to me, Felicia: Do not lie to yourself, either. If he ever comes here to the office —"

"Oh, he will never come here," Felicia spurted, waving her hands in an X shape. "He is afraid of you."

"He should be." She tugged on her London Fog overcoat and clutched her Coach purse, weighted by the pistol in it. A fire engine screamed past, and as usual, she paused and worried that the car or home involved might be one of her clients.

"I'll call in later," she said at the door. She tapped her eyebrow. "And put some ice on that, OK? Leave early if you need to."

"*Gracias, Señorita* Selena," the receptionist said.

Selena crossed to the garage, breathing hard, indignant, her three-inch Lumianis pounding the pavement. Men can be such pigs. Where did they get the idea that it was *macho* to strike a woman? Her own brother Lorenzo had left a trail of battered girlfriends behind him, and when he drank — well, it was just a good thing he'd never raised a hand to her. She knew exactly where to kick her pointed Pradas.

In the garage, she stripped the navy-blue tarp from the Charger with a single sweep, letting the fabric and fleece lining tumble away like a collapsing cloud. Bragg's interruption prevented her from testing the new pipes. A drive-around would give some sense of the job, listening for rattles, hearing the roar. But she'd have to drop into Performance Plus to check for an evap-system leak using their smoke-machine flow gauge, like that time Antonio returned from his Frankfurt motor pool service on furlough, right around this time of year.

"Do you smell anything back there?" Antonio had asked, waving the torque wrench.

"I smell something," Selena said near the right tailpipe. "Something kinda sweet."

"It's not from the car," Antonio said with a laugh. "Just the neighbors burning leaves."

"It stinks."

"It should smell more like rubber," he said.

She passed her nose along the chassis. "Nothing."

"OK, I'll run an evap test with the scan tool. Step back and don't touch anything."

She stood behind Antonio while he connected cables for an in-bay test.

"If this doesn't work, I'll need a smoke machine for a split-system check," Antonio said. "Then maybe use a C-25 gas charge. I already have a bottle of it for the MIG welder."

Selena sniffed. "Hey, turn your head this way."

"What?"

"This way." She pulled his chin.

He swatted away her hand. "*¿Qué húbole?*"

"What's up with *you*?" she said. "That smell is coming from *you*."

"What are you talkin' about, *pico de águila?*"

Eagle beak. If it had been someone else, she would have broken his nose. "It's marijuana."

"Nah, it's the leaves," he said, leaning into the engine.

"Cannabis leaves," she said. "How long you been doing this?"

"Doing what?"

"Don't mess with me." She punched his shoulder. "You doin' anything else? Meth? You're awfully thin."

"Do you mind?" he said, turning away. "I gotta calibrate the machine, and it takes some math."

"How about this math: three to five for possession of a controlled substance."

"What are you now: DEA or somethin'?"

"If *Mamí* finds out, you'll break her heart."

"Look, *cuate*, it's just weed. It relaxes me, OK? You should see what some of the guys flying into the post from Afghanistan are doing to deal with their crap."

"Who are you getting it from?"

"Back off, sis. I'll be OK. Really. Don't worry about it. It's safer than drinking. Now help me connect this to the purge valve, will ya?"

He was dead in a month.

At the station, the dead men's mug shots were taped to the whiteboard, with the date, time, place, and manner of death scribbled with colored Expo markers beside them. Maps of Illinois and metro Chicago hung by push pins along the cork strip at the top, the killing locations circled. A calendar was taped along the bottom, with an X on each victim's date.

"What's the pattern so far, besides our list?" Selena asked.

"He started in Chicago," Bragg said, "in early August. The next few are in Chicagoland, as you'd expect. Here, here, here, and here." He tapped the map locations with the eraser end of a pencil. "Then he worked his way west to Rockford, then south, with a detour here and there, on his way to you, the last stop."

Selena imagined a line connecting the spots. It looked like a snake, striking from a coiled position. "And about every two weeks, you said?"

Gordon lifted a coffee mug. "That's right."

"The funny thing," Selena observed, "is that he starts in mid-August, not November. Why doesn't he wait until November 2, The Day of the Dead, when he goes public with the list in The Book of the Deceased?"

"It's a mystery," Gordon acknowledged dryly.

Selena tapped her temple, toggling a memory. "When did Jacinta first encounter The Blue Lady? August, wasn't it?"

Bragg said it was.

"The first hit is August 16," Selena thought aloud. "The Feast of the Assumption is the 15th. Religious feelings would run high. That must be the date of the first apparition and prediction. I'll check with Father Johnny."

"The first few guys got no warning," Gordon said. "Too bad."

"Maybe the book is an afterthought," Bragg offered. "The Day of the Dead approaches, and he gets the idea late. Hey, he thinks, not only can I pop these guys when they don't see it coming, but even when they do. It's also his chance to brag who's behind it all, taunting us at the same time."

"The book is all we have?" Selena asked.

Bragg threw his hands up. "We've tracked down all former residences. We've checked phone numbers, credit cards, license plates. We think he's using disposable phones and stolen credit cards. Illinois State Police are on alert for him. We checked bank accounts and bank surveillance cameras. Nothing. It's like he isn't even in the country. We've shown his photo around everywhere, and no one has seen him. So they say. Not everyone wants to talk to us."

"Our only connection is this girl Jacinta and her Blue Lady," Gordon said. "She knows something she isn't telling us."

"It's not that," Selena snapped. "She just doesn't know the importance of what she knows. It's not like she was holding out on us like some doper would."

"Yeah, well, I'm not so sure," Gordon grumped, scratching at his military crewcut.

"You know, Selena, she looks a little like that girl you shot," Bragg said.

Selena bristled. "Do all brown people look the same to you?"

"Hey, wait a minute, I was only saying —"

"I know what you were saying."

"All I know," Gordon butt in, "is that I'd like for you to talk to her again. On her own turf. And, if possible, away from that aunt of hers, Sandoval."

Selena puffed her nostrils. "I plan to," she said. "Do you have the aunt's address?"

"Sure do," Gordon replied. "I'll get it."

He stood, walked to a vertical file and fingered through a drawer.

Bragg stroked his chin and planted himself on a desk's edge. He drummed the pencil on his palm. "You know what, Selena? I've got a plan."

She groaned inwardly. The gung-ho Army Ranger hated the hunting game and the waiting game. 'Go in with guns blazing' was his usual plan.

Like the raid on a house where there was a woman who'd been robbed not long before, who thought she was being burglarized again and met the officers with a .38 Special she had bought for home protection. They shot her dead. No drugs in the house except prescription ibuprofen for her arthritis.

Then there was the elderly man who died of a heart attack from the shock of the pre-dawn assault. His middle-school grandson, who was sleeping over, had only a little stale marijuana that Grandpa didn't even know about.

And the raid with the girl. And the merciless headlines afterward. COCAINE COWGIRL SUSPENDED. DEA SHOOTER HAD

HISTORY OF WRITE-UPS. FEDS BUST BUSTED. LATINOS UNIDOS PROTESTERS DEMAND RESIGNATION. MARCHERS CALL FOR END TO RAIDS. And the lawsuits. And the reporters at the door. *Do you always shoot first and ask questions later? How does it feel to shoot one of your own?*

And Bragg's warning not to break the blue wall of silence when these matters went to court, where the raids were justified and the families paid off with generous settlements.

Selena folded her arms. "A plan, huh?"

"Instead of us finding him, let him find us."

She narrowed her eyes, suspicious. "What do you mean?"

"The district office has been running this drug house over in Bison Grove," he said. "And if we can get a rumor going of a sweet enough deal there, he might show up."

"What kind of deal?"

"I'll take you there," he said, evasive. "There's someone there I want you to meet. We'll talk it over then. Get your coat."

"Later," Selena said. "First I want to visit Eva Sandoval and try to talk to Jacinta and see if she's OK."

Gordon answered a trilling phone. "Yeah, they're still here," he said. He cupped the receiver. *Coroner*, he mouthed. "What's that? Huh? No kidding? Sure, I'll tell them."

He hung up and blew out a sigh.

"Autopsy results?" Bragg asked. "What did she find?"

"It's what she didn't find," Gordon said. "The heart is missing."

CHAPTER 12

She hates getting milked.

From the minute I pin her spade-shaped head to the sandy vivarium bottom with the T-stick to the moment my thumb and finger squeeze the quadrate bones of her so-called shoulders to lift her out, she twists. Twists like crazy. When she's tired, I grab her tail and let the stick drop away. I tuck her under my arm, and she unfolds those hypodermic fangs from the roof of her mouth and I can see the straw-colored neurotoxin already pearling on the tips.

She's really mad now. Her tail wants to vibrate, but I've got it good and snug. That's it — hiss a little. Drip a little more. Into the dish. There. Good girl. I'll make it worth your while.

When she's done, I fling her head down into the box and snap the lid shut. She coils into a tight spiral attitude, alert and defensive, tongue flicking, trying to sense the location of my hand. I was too slow once. Just once. Good thing I had the antivenin nearby. My hand was the size of a catcher's mitt for a week.

After I peel off the goggles, I pour the lovely leche into a glass Mason jar and seal it. It gets a label that only I can read and a spot behind the imported long-stem roses in the fridge. It's ready for the next time if I want to use it.

The others are curling up in their boxes against the walls that are closest to the hot-water pipes, now that the first light of day is turning the ceiling panes from black to gray. Except for a couple of locals, they're all night hunters. The deserts where they come from are too hot in the daytime to do anything but sleep. The Mexican moccasin, the eyelash viper, the palm viper, all of them. Except

Viper

that nervous *barba amarilla*. He hunts anytime. Even when he isn't hungry. I never milk him. One bite and you're dead.

Too bad I couldn't use him for that low-life dealer last night. The *barba* is just too big to carry around. The Mexican viper worked just fine. The guy reaches in the canvas bag to get his cash and — surprise. Shocks him just long enough for me to cut his throat. Scum. He bled a lot after the second cut just below the ribs.

So I have what I promised you. It's a little bigger than my fist but you've swallowed things that size before. I've rubbed it in the anal waste of the red diamondback, just as you like it.

I hold it in the long forceps and offer it through the door of the trap box. Her tongue gets busy, smelling it. She uncoils into the S position. She's still mad.

CHAPTER 13

Selena drove The Beast up to Eva Sandoval's tenement, parallel parking behind a late-model Honda. She had expected a beat-up *barrio* but instead found a neighborhood of tidy brick row houses, some in decent shape, some needing a little love. The Hispanic population was officially one or two percent in this town but about to explode with the arrival of agri-businesses swallowing up family farms and needing laborers. No doubt some of these flats — even some garages and attics — were packed with uncounted and undocumented immigrants hoping for those jobs. Selena would have to be careful to say she wanted only to check on Jacinta apart from the *Anglo* cops and she had no interest in examining anyone's papers.

The rumbling Charger always gained street cred in *Latino* neighborhoods like this where low riders thumped to Chicano rap and Aztlan hip-hop. When she cut the engine and stepped out, she noticed all the brown faces pulling aside curtains to trace the sound of thunder. *Too many young men*, she thought. *Idle or high school dropouts. We've got to do something about that.*

She tugged her black trench coat tighter. The air was damp, muffling the sound of Tejano music with its skipping accordion and foot-dragging bass. She took a deep breath and the smell of someone making *tamales* gave her a boost of determination. It was Mexican comfort food, although she knew *gringos* who said it smelled like sweaty feet. The mouth-watering aroma could be coming from the Fiesta Market or the *Iglesia Cristo Vive* across the street.

She double-checked the street address on a card Detective Gordon had given her.

It's very difficult to prove abuse, you know, he had cautioned her. *The girl said she was beaten. We've got to get her out of there.*

I told you, Miss De La Cruz, I can't intervene.

OK, so if I see anything funny, bruises or welts, I'll call the Illinois Department of Children and Family Services, and they can send their own investigator, Selena told him. *They can question her, find witnesses, and make her go to a physician to give her an exam and look for evidence of abuse.*

I don't want DCFS to mess up my investigation, Gordon said. *Don't you mess it up, either. When you go over there, just ask her about The Blue Lady.*

Selena tucked away the card, strode confidently up the steps to the porch, and rapped on the front door. She stepped away from it and stood off at an angle.

No sense in getting shot through the door.

She folded her arms and waited. She had no warrant, just the gold shield on hand to flash at the woman if she thought it necessary. But why blow her civilian cover? It may be best to remain the conscientious local insurance agent, the handy translator. Maybe she should apologize for reacting harshly, or say she had come representing the Sinnissippi Literacy Council, for whom she did language instruction, and offer to tutor Jacinta. Yes, that was it. She knocked again.

The deadbolt slid back, and the door creaked open. Eva Sandoval scratched her ear. "You," she said in Spanish. "You want to see Jacinta, don't you?"

"As a matter of fact, I —"

"She's gone, as usual," Eva complained, her heavily shadowed eyes turned skyward, flicking her hand. "She's run off to who-knows-where this time. Look, *chica,* I'm sorry I came down on you so hard. Please forgive me. I should have thanked you for finding her. I told you she's sick and needs help. I'm just trying to be a good aunt to her, you know, since her mother is dead, my dear sister, and her dad was deported and — well, maybe you don't know how it is, being well off. I mean — well, look at you." She pointed to Selena's shoes.

The Christian Louboutin patent platform pumps peeked from the cuffs of her black Guess jeans, and Selena felt her cheeks pinking.

It had always been hard to explain that her dad had been the lucky immigrant, the oil executive who got a good job in Chicago's Mexican Consulate so he could raise his children as American citizens. Class envy cut across race lines.

Eva put her palm to her heart. "I'm actually relieved it's you because DCFS has been trying to take Jacinta away from me, and all I want to do is get her to go to school and get some counseling, you know, maybe at Catholic Charities, where you can pay in empty pop cans, did you know that? But how can I do that if she keeps running off and has all these crazies protecting her? Tell me that."

"I'm sorry, but I can't —"

"And speaking of school, I'm going full-time up at the community college to better myself, to start a business someday and maybe give Jacinta a life, you know?" She counted on her fingers. "Anthropology, economics, flower-arranging, business math — you think this is easy?" Her eyes were lined, weary. Selena saw the struggle written on her face.

"No, I —"

"Well, it isn't. Anyway, if you cops find her, let me know and I'll pick her up again."

"I'm not a cop," Selena said, producing a business card.

Sandoval took it. "An insurance agent? You here to sell me something?"

"Call me if Jacinta comes home. I tutor English with the local literacy council, at the River Falls Public Library, and maybe I can help get her back into school. And I have a therapist as an insurance client. I could talk to her about helping Jacinta."

"Fine. I appreciate that —" she glanced at the card. "Miss De La Cruz. I'll be in touch. The therapist sounds like a good idea. I'm so worried for her. When I heard she was at the police station, I thought she'd been arrested for using drugs. Maybe that's why I was so angry. Maybe that's why she's having these — these so-called visions. You know what's out there on the streets."

She did. She nodded in sympathy.

"Thank you for understanding," Eva said. "*Adios.*"

Selena looked past the woman as the door closed, the sweet perfume of roses suddenly noticeable. Selena had forgotten how Mexican homes, no matter how poor, were full of freshly cut blooms.

She made her way back to her car, wondering at the woman's switched personality. It was perfectly understandable if she'd been angry and anxious about the possibility of Jacinta's using drugs. Lord knows there was plenty of cheap junk on the streets, psychedelics and deliriants that caused dreamy trances and visions.

She slipped into the Charger and brought it to life. With nothing substantial to report to Gordon or Bragg, she'd return to the office. No need to have her receptionist Felicia wonder too much about what she was doing on the side.

She merged into the highway flow, pondering the drug angle. If someone was giving Jacinta substances to promote a devotion to this Blue Lady, maybe Eva Sandoval had good reason to be angry.

"Do not be angry with me," squeaked a little voice in Spanish.

Selena swung the car into the breakdown lane and stopped with a jerk. Was she hearing voices, too? *Madre de Dios*, she whispered.

She turned and looked down.

Jacinta squatted in the passenger side well.

"Can you take me home with you now?" the girl asked sweetly. "The men are not here who say you cannot."

Selena sucked in her breath, heart pummeling. How had she not seen her? How had she not heard the car door open and shut while she was on the stoop? "Jacinta, what are you doing?"

"You said you would come," Jacinta said. "I knew you would keep your promise, *Señorita* Selena."

"I did," Selena answered, "but I cannot take you to my home."

"You did not say no before."

"Well, I'm saying it now."

The fawn eyes filled with tears. "*¿Por que?*"

"Because it is against the law," Selena said. "You must be in your own home."

"Do not take me back, please do not," she said, folding her hands in entreaty. "My *tía*, she will not understand —"

"You aunt cares for you and is confused about the things you do," Selena said.

An eighteen-wheeler screamed by, shaking the car.

"This is not a good place to talk," Selena said, shifting to drive. "Are you hungry? I'll take you to lunch, and we can talk there. Would you like that?"

Jacinta fingered away a tear and nodded. *"Sí."*

"Get up into the seat and fasten the seat belt, ok? Good girl."

The girl obeyed. Once Selena heard the buckle click, she eased into the traffic and took the next exit, where a Burger Barn sign appeared. Unsure of what to do with the girl afterward, she parked, her mind racing with questions to ask.

She opened the door for Jacinta and took her by the hand into the restaurant.

"What is it you would like?" Selena asked the girl.

Jacinta studied the back-lit menu photos above the ordering counter. "That one," she indicated.

"I like that one, too," Selena said.

"I would like to use the bathroom first," Jacinta said.

"It's over there," Selena said, releasing the girl's hand.

"Who's next? Step up, please," called the order-taker in the bright red cap.

Selena placed the order, requesting coffee for herself and a chocolate milk for Jacinta. She selected a table and glanced around at the busy lunch crowd, relieved that no one seemed abuzz about Jacinta's presence. Then again, most of the clientele was Anglo. *Once we're seated, I'll check her skin for bruises and get a better look at her eyes.* She wouldn't ask directly about drug use, but there were other ways to find out, short of a blood test or a "drop." Too bad she couldn't collect the sample Jacinta was leaving in the ladies' room right now.

"Number 86!" the counter help shouted.

Selena retrieved the tray and sat down. She uncapped the coffee and blew on it. She took a tentative sip; it was hot. She could use the restroom, too.

Oh, no. She set down the cup and made a bee-line for the lavatory. *Not a good idea to let her go in there alone,* she reprimanded herself.

She pushed inside. The girl wasn't at the sinks. Selena called her name, bent low, and checked the stalls. No feet. She kicked open every stall door. No Jacinta. Selena rushed into the restaurant and examined the crowd. Not there. She burst out the glass doors into the parking lot. Checked her car. Banged her fist on the roof.

Jacinta had vanished.

CHAPTER 14

"Have you dumped Rick yet?" Bragg asked.

"Reed," Selena corrected him. "And no. I'm keeping our date tomorrow. I'll tell him then."

Bragg angled the Tahoe to the curb and parked. "Be sure you do," he said. "I don't want any leaks, and you don't want him hurt. Especially now that our guy is playing Jack the Ripper."

"I understand," she replied, resigned, her chest hollow.

"Good. Then let's go inside."

They stepped out and strode up the cement walk to the rickety front steps of the rental house. Selena side-stepped brown slush. She should have worn the old Payless pumps. At the porch, ignoring the smell of ripe garbage from the alley, she studied the nearby two-story tenements with barbeques and bikes and hip-hop thumping somewhere. Student neighborhood. Bragg rapped a code on the door with his heavy ring. The peephole opened, shut, and the door ca-clicked open.

"Good day, sir," said the officer dressed in jeans, flannel shirt, and a down vest. The clipped speech gave him away.

"Hello, Dawes," Bragg acknowledged him. "Is Baker with him?"

"In the kitchen."

"This way, Selena."

She followed Bragg through the living room decorated in vintage Goodwill, cluttered with laundry, crushed Mountain Dew cans, dirty dishes, and other student debris. A tabby cat slinked under the ratty couch. In the kitchen, the other officer in a White Sox jacket and khakis sat at a Formica-topped table with a young Latino slouched across from him. The teenager, 18 or so, was dressed in a gray hooded sweatshirt with an *Aeropostale* logo. The hood was down, and a barbed wire tattoo poked from the collar. The lifted heel of his right Converse sneaker moved up and down to a beat he heard in his head, a nervous tic. The mustache below his aquiline nose looked like a thin shadow, and the sideburns were shaven to sharp points near his taut lips. He didn't bother to stand when a woman entered the room. A lost custom, a crude *machismo*.

The officer swiveled and extended his burly hand to Selena. "I'm Baker, ma'am," he said. "I've heard a lot about you."

"Any of it good?" she asked, squeezing the hand.

"Yes, ma'am," he said, shaking his fingers, the smile gone. "Hey, that's quite a grip for a lady."

"I'm no lady," Selena said. She nodded to the sullen young man. "*¿Oye, qué onda?*"

"Not much," he said. "Whassup with you?"

She shrugged. "*Eh, lo mismo.*" She took a seat. His cacao eyes hungrily followed her down into it.

"*Me llamo Selena,*" she introduced herself.

"I know who you are." He sniffed. The heel moved faster.

Bragg turned a chair around and squatted across it, arms folded on the backrest. "Glad you two have met. Miguel here has been working with our drug house set-up for three months over in Bison Grove," he said. "We supply good stuff, guys come for it, he helps us to identify the guys we get on camera."

"OK, a basic sting op," Selena said.

"Not so basic anymore. One of the customers was that guy killed in the cemetery."

"*Zurramato,*" Miguel said under his breath.

"That wasn't his name," Bragg corrected.

"The word means a lazy and ugly moron," Selena said. "Go ahead."

Bragg reddened. "The name was Rodríguez. Anyway, Miguel says the guy bragged about knowing The Snake and probably talked to him about our little house. So he knows about it. We think we have a chance to get him to come to the house and take him down before he can get anyone else on that list." He winked at her.

"Why should he come?" she asked Miguel. "For good *bazuco*?"

"*Oye*, he gets plenty of that elsewhere," he said.

"I see," Selena said. "Then it's because he'd want to shut you down like the others, to eliminate the competition."

"He might," Bragg interjected. "But the only way to make sure he comes is by offering, shall we say, bigger bait."

Her insides knotted.

Bragg grinned.

"You mean me," she said.

"Miguel here thinks he can make contact with The Snake through the friends of the guy who got popped," Bragg said. "He'll say he's met you and that you're coming to close a deal on a particular day and time. He'll act real proud about it. The Snake will probably scold him for being set up by a woman, and he won't be able to resist showing up at the same time to — well, you know."

Selena leaned back in the chair and crossed her legs. She stared at Bragg. He smiled back. She knew him well. Rather than have Miguel take them to The Snake, it would be safer for The Snake to come to her, and smarter to have control of the space.

Selena turned and drilled Miguel with her eyes. "Why should The Snake believe you when you say it's me coming to you?"

He pointed to her silver Miu Miu high heels with the bow ties.

"*Los zapatos*," he said. "I'll tell him about your shoes."

CHAPTER 15

Selena lowered the Zeiss binoculars, shook her silken hair back, and searched the tree line with a gloved hand over her brow. "I don't see her."

Reed Stubblefield pointed to the highest branch of the bare hickory on the river island. "There she is," he said. Reed hugged Selena's shoulders from behind and steered her to the left two degrees. Her leather bombardier jacket squeaked. "How about now?"

She focused the eyepieces and drew in a sharp breath. She had spotted the eagle.

"She's beautiful," she whispered.

"The male can't be far away," Reed said with a glance about, one hand shading his eyes. "Goldens hunt in pairs. One drives the prey to its waiting partner."

"Oh!" Selena exclaimed. "There she goes."

The eagle plunged to the shimmering river like a bolt, dropped its talons into the water, and flapped up. A fish wriggled in its iron grip. The mate, wheeling high above in a spiraling column of warm air, swooped down with a triumphant screech to join her in the eyrie.

Selena handed back the binoculars, a palm to her chest. "*Madrecita*, they're so strong and fast," she said, breathless, "and lovely. I can see why you're so taken with them."

"They're excellent hunters and, as you can see, not bad at fishing, either," Reed agreed. "But the thing I really like about them is that they mate for life."

Her heart pounded — with dread. *Don't go there. He wouldn't. Would he? Change the subject.*

"Do you have an appointment with Dr. Rashidi while you're in town?" she asked. "It's been almost six months, right?"

He arched an eyebrow, taken aback. "Yes. As a matter of fact, I do. Tomorrow. He's still not ready to call my hip a miracle just because I don't need the cane anymore — to the disappointment of anyone who wants Father Ray declared a saint."

Talk of the case of the stigmatic priest still buzzed in the bars and byways of River Falls, and of Reed's apparent healing of his gunshot-shattered hip.

Not even a hairline fracture to be seen, Dr. Rashidi had marveled. *It's almost as though it never happened. I don't understand.*

I don't understand that I may believe, but I believe that I may understand, according to Thomas Aquinas, Reed had quoted.

He laughed. "Dr. Rashidi shrugs his shoulders and my regular doctor in Chicago will only say that it is inexplicable."

"I think that's all the Church needs to advance Father Ray's cause for beatification," Selena said.

"Speaking of Chicago," Reed replied, the peaceful sea-gray eyes exploring her own, suddenly looking stormy, "driving back and forth on weekends to see you isn't working, Selena, and I — well, I'm — well —"

Her heart took another skip. Was he breaking up instead? Giving her an out? Did she really want that? She squared her shoulders and nodded. "I understand, and I don't blame you," she said with a confident sweep of her hand. "It isn't working at all." Her stomach clenched. She didn't mean it.

"I'm glad you agree," he said with the warm smile that always melted her heart. "That's why I've accepted an adjunct instructor position at Sinnissippi Community College here in town, starting in January."

She tensed. "What?"

"With a few upgrades to my brother's hunting cabin, I can stay in River Falls all season. All year."

"You — you shouldn't," she said, her mind spinning. "I mean, not now. Not until January. When school starts. Don't you think? Wouldn't that be — logical?"

His eyes narrowed into a puzzled look. The creases added wisdom to his handsome face.

"Well, it isn't as though I'll be paying for two places," he said, working through the logic. "Dan will be glad for me to keep his place up over the winter."

She lowered her chin. "It isn't that. I —"

"What's wrong?"

"I won't be here," she lied. "It's the slow season for insurance. People buy homes and cars in late spring, in better weather, and so I'm — I'll be out of town. A lot. Especially weekends. Conferences. License certification training. At the company headquarters in Iowa."

Why was she stammering? Didn't she lie to armed dopers without a blink? Flick her hand at Lady Death a dozen times?

Reed cocked his head. "But during the week, your business —"

"I have a team of independent adjusters to handle claims," she cut in. "And I visit family in Mexico over the holidays. All of them: Thanksgiving, *Posada*, Our Lady of Guadalupe. I've done it for years. I just — I just won't be able to see you." It wasn't entirely a lie. If she could just keep him out of the way for a few weeks.

"I see," he replied. "Well, if that's the way you want it —"

"It isn't, really," she said, forcing a smile. "It's just the way it has to be. For a while."

"Until when?"

"I'll let you know."

He furrowed his brow, pensive. No, *suspicious*. "Are you sure there isn't something else you want to tell me?"

"Positively." That was true. There was plenty she didn't want to tell him. Not yet.

"If you change your mind," Reed said, "I'll still be visiting town a few times to meet with my mentor at the college."

"You?" she questioned. "You need a mentor after all your years of teaching?"

He laughed. "Every part-time adjunct is assigned a full-timer to learn the ropes of the school — how to file forms, where the copier is, correct wording for the syllabi, and so on. We'll learn from each other, I hope. We were matched due to our mutual interest in mythology. I know the Greek material; he's a Meso-American expert."

"Meso-American?"

"Sure. You know — Toltec, Mayan. Aztec."

Selena seized on the word. "Aztec?" she repeated.

"You should see his office. It's full of artifacts from archaeological diggings he does with students over the winter break in Mexico."

"What's his name again?"

"Salazar," Reed said. "Jorge Salazar. Someone you know?"

Someone I probably need to know, she thought. "Doesn't ring a bell," she said. "Tell him I can get him a deal on travel insurance for student trips." She tucked in her scarf and then took his hand. She laced her fingers in his. "Can we go, *cariño*? I'm getting chilly. Let's get a hot chocolate somewhere, OK?"

"Sure. Sure, we can do that." He studied her face, still suspicious. "Nothing I need to know?"

"Nothing." *Tell him nothing, Bragg said. Nothing.*

Another eagle screeched, dove to the water, raked the surface, and flew off with a kill.

"I'm just finishing an early lunch," Jorge Salazar said, dabbing a napkin at his mouth and bristly mustache. "Come in. What can I do for you? You're not in any of my classes, are you? Have a question about the spring schedule?"

"Only if you're teaching Aztec mythology," Selena answered, stepping into the glass-enclosed office. She surveyed the framed Meso-American posters: an Aztec calendar stone, a view of the Mexican pyramids at dusk, a warrior in an eagle mask wielding a fearsome club. Two Toltec statues, squat and severe, served as bookends for anthropology textbooks. Artifacts poked from piles of papers atop the file cabinet. Pottery. A wood flute. A jagged obsidian knife. Just as Reed had described.

"Souvenirs," Salazar said, noticing her perusal. "I put the real arti-facts in the art gallery or the department showcase in Humanities Hall. Please, have a seat."

"Archaeological work?" Selena asked, lowering herself into the fabric chair.

"I go to Mexico every winter break," Salazar said. "The weather's better then, and I can get some good digging done with a few interns who come along for academic credit and to improve their Spanish. Here's one now."

A young woman, clad in Goth black with shiny blue toenails peeping from her sandals, paused outside the door. "Oh — is this a good time? It's your office hour, isn't it?"

"This will just take a moment," he told Selena. "What can I do for you, Alicia?"

The young woman reached into a hemp tote bag decorated in the festive tricolor of the Mexican flag. Her razor-cut hair, dyed blue, fell in a graceful arc around her face, framing it and giving it an azure cast. She stood straight, swished back her hair, and handed over a sheet. "I brought the gallery inventory list you asked for, Professor."

Salazar took it and gave it a quick glance. "*Gracias*, Alicia. This is a big help."

Alicia turned to Selena. "Are you signing up for the Winter Break Excavation? I could tell you all about it. I went last year, and it was super."

"No, I just came for some basic course information. I'm interested in Aztec culture."

"Oh," Alicia said, the dark eyebrows lifted, onyx eyes widened. "The Aztecs had, like, this really awesome civilization. Art, agricul-ture, astronomy, architecture, poetry — I mean, like, they had these *huuuge* speaking contests where they recited their history and poems in public for days. Even the name of the language, Nahuatl, means 'elegant speech.' "

Maybe she was showing off for her instructor.

"I had no idea," Selena replied.

"Most people don't," she said, crimping her mouth. "Not even Mexicans. They just don't know their own heritage at all and have forgotten, like, everything. Especially everything about the gods and goddesses who gave them rain and crops and babies and music and protection from enemies, like the Feathered Serpent. The Catholic Church took care of that."

"Didn't the Catholic Church also put an end to human sacrifice?" Selena rejoined.

"Was that a *good* thing?" Alicia asked sourly.

Selena did a double take. "How is that a *bad* thing?"

Alicia glanced at her professor with a smirk. "Consider: As long as the Aztecs made their offerings, their culture flourished. Once they stopped, their great civilization collapsed and their great achievements were forgotten."

Was she echoing something Salazar had said in class?

"Anything else, Joe?" Alicia asked, her chin high.

"This will do, *gracias*," Salazar said, tapping the page.

"OK," she said, pivoting to exit. She stopped, spun, and giggled. "Didja hear, Joe? She made an appearance again a few days ago. Made another prediction."

Salazar shook his head and gave a little laugh. "Don't tell me — another punk showed up dead the next day in a cemetery."

"How'd you guess?" she said with a playful pout. "See you in class."

Alicia left.

"You're talking about the visionary who sees The Blue Lady?" Selena asked.

"So you've heard of her?" Salazar said. "That poor little girl. Probably mentally ill, wouldn't you think?"

Selena shrugged. "I wouldn't know. You're not a believer, I take it?"

"Let me put it this way," he said, assuming a professorial tone. "We are in a season of the traditional Mexican year that celebrates the harvest of grains and the harvest of human souls, especially in the festival called The Day of the Dead. You know this, right? So you also know the Spanish *conquistadores* absorbed it into All Souls' Day but the peoples of *Mexica* kept their customs that celebrate the cycle of life and death. So I say that if it is anyone at all appearing to that poor girl, it is *Mictecacihuatl* herself, the Aztec goddess of death. It's as plausible as saying it is Our Lady of Guadalupe."

"You really think so?"

"What I *really* think is that Juan Diego, the peasant who claimed to see the Virgin, is a convenient fiction invented by the Catholic Church, a story told to the Indians to convert them from devotion to *Tonantzín*, an Aztec fertility goddess. Small wonder, then, that the Virgin's image is of a pregnant princess."

He crumpled wax paper with the leftover crusts from a tuna sandwich and tossed it into a trash can. "Did you have a specific question? I need to get to class."

"I think you've answered my questions," Selena said.

CHAPTER 16

When Selena wheeled the Charger onto 18th Street in Chicago's Pilsen neighborhood, the throaty rumble of the big engine turned the heads of young men in tilted White Sox caps. In the air, *Norteño* bands playing plaintive *corridos* on button accordions competed with the thump-thump of *quebradita*, a blend of North Mexican *banda* and Aztec punk rockers singing in Spanglish. Selena felt her Spanish blood beating.

She crossed herself and kissed her thumb and forefinger held together when she passed Saint Adalbert's Elementary in the shadow of the church's skyline-dominating steeple. In the sixth grade, Sister Mary Beatrice — whom every kid called Sister Mary BattleAxe — caught Selena speaking Spanish in the back row. She was asking Gloria García for an eraser. Sister pulled Selena by the ear into the corner.

"You're in America now," the Polish nun had reprimanded, her milky finger in Selena's mocha face. "We speak English here. If you want to be an American, speak American. If you want to speak Spanish, then go back to Mexico."

Selena asked if there was a difference between speaking English and speaking American.

Sister Beatrice kept her after school for talking back.

"*Ay*, you don't talk back," her mother chided her when she got home. *Mami's* high Zapotec cheekbones colored like the red-hot lava of Mount Popocatépetl, and the obsidian-black bun on top of her head, Selena could have sworn, was spinning.

"*Muchachitas bien criadas*, girls brought up well, don't mouth off," her mother said, wringing the dish towel. "Do you want to be called *habladora*? A big mouth that talks too much? Is that what you want?"

"*Mami*, all I did was ask a question."

"*En boca cerrada no entran moscas,*" her mother said, tapping her lips with a finger. *Flies cannot enter a closed mouth.* "You must be quiet, and keep your eyes low in *respeto*, like *La Virgen de Guadalupe.*"

Selena did not tell her what the kids did in recess the next day. Joey Kowalski asked her if she knew the Frito Bandito and got the others to dance around a hat, singing "La Cucaracha" while snapping their fingers like castanets over their heads. How could they know the famous Pancho Villa song was about Mexican heroes who bravely fought back against white oppressors? So when Joey asked her if she knew Speedy Gonzalez, too, and trilled *"¡Ándale! ¡Ándale! ¡Arriba! ¡Arriba!"* Selena bloodied his nose with a single punch. He was too astonished and ashamed to tell Sister Mary BattleAxe what had really happened and said he had taken a direct hit in the face during dodge ball in recess.

She told Antonio that night.

"The boxing lessons I gave you, they helped, *no?*" he said, laughing. "Did you put your shoulder into it, the way I showed you, like this?"

"Stop it," Selena whispered, deflecting the playful punch. "*Mami* says I already act too much like you boys. Promise you won't tell her. Or Lorenzo or Francisco. Promise."

"OK, Oscar de la Hoya."

"It's not funny. And don't tell *Papá*, either."

"Oh, he might be glad," Antonio chuckled. "He wanted nine boys to start his own *béisbol* team. Then you came along and put a stop to that idea."

She socked him in the shoulder; he swung the pillow into her face, she threw hers at him, and soon the room was full of giggles and pillow stuffing.

But after that, Selena decided to tell Comadre María, her favorite aunt and godmother, during her weekly visit. How long ago was it when she took the bus and skipped down this very sidewalk in the pleated uniform skirt and saddle shoes to share her joys and sorrows with her wise *tía*? Comadre María always understood.

As she would now.

A powdery snow dusted the murals on the buildings' sides, a mix of Polish and Mexican art to rival the galleries on Halsted Street. When Selena parked in front of the bright blue townhouse, she noticed the yellow window boxes were culled of geraniums and petunias. *Madrina* María kept up the little garden in back where the *gruta* shrine, tucked in the corner, held the plaster Virgin Mary, a smaller statue of Saint Anthony and a fading photograph of her brother Antonio. By now, the bright yellow *cempasuchil* garlands from the Day of the Dead would be brittle, the cross of orange marigolds browned by the bitter breath of an approaching winter. Plastic ferns and silk wreaths from a dollar store kept up appearances until the spring thaw brought back the Sacred Heart irises, Mary's Tears, Roses of Guadalupe and, of course, the herbs. Selena braced herself for her godmother's complaints about having to buy some in the local *barrista*, where the German grocers had switched from Polish merchandise to Mexican when the neighborhood changed.

Selena found her in the Puebla-tiled kitchen putting away groceries while an *Univision telenovela* on the countertop TV babbled in the background.

"*Hola, Selena, pequeña hija,*" the old woman said warmly, arms outstretched. "I always know it is you coming. I can hear you a kilometer away. When will you get that old car fixed?"

Selena hugged her, kissed both cheeks, and smiled. "*Dentro de poco*, soon, *Madrina.*"

"*Ay*, how you and Antonio worked so much on it, and it only got louder," she reminisced. "Maybe you should sell it."

"Someday, *Madrina*. Here, let me help you. I'm sorry I am late and couldn't help with the shopping as usual. My meetings went so long."

"*Cada uno lleva su cruz,*" she replied with the familiar proverb. Everyone carries his own cross. "I am so sorry for you. You must be very tired. Poor dear. Sit, sit. I'll do this."

"No, let me. I'll take that." Selena took the Spice Islands bottle of cilantro from her hand.

"*Ay*, see how I must buy dried-up cilantro flakes in a little bottle. And the price, so high. Put it here by the stove."

Selena stored the *manzanilla* tea, *fideo* pasta, pork loin, black *frijoles*, and Mexican coffee in all the usual spots while her *Madrina* pulled a ceramic bowl from a shelf.

"You must be hungry, *querida*," Comadre María said, gripping Selena's arm and squeezing it in two places. "*Ay*, how skinny. No wonder you don't have a man yet. I'll make something. Put the pot of beans on the stove for me, and find my favorite pan. You know the one."

Comadre María poured flour into the bowl for the *tortillas*, felt the amount with her fingers, and then spooned in baking powder. She added salt by hand in the shape of a cross to bless it. "So — tell me about your week, child," she said, kneading.

"I'm not supposed to tell anyone," Selena said.

"*En boca cerrada no entran moscas*, it is true," Comadre María answered, her unmoving eyes fixed straight ahead. "But if you stay silent, child, how then can I pray for you?"

Selena cupped her chin in her palm and sighed. "You remember how I worked with drug enforcement?"

"And how your mother hated it. God rest her soul, she said you would never find a man, and you would end up *una solterona*, an old maid, as long as you carried a gun and acted like a boy. Thanks be to God, you left and now have an honorable business your *Papá* would be proud of."

"They want me back."

The woman stopped patting the dough. "And you would do this?"

"Only for a short while. As a consultant. They need what I know." It was the best explanation. "With my old boss. Who is as bad as ever."

"*No juzgues el hombre por su vestido*," Comadre María recited. Do not judge a man by what he's wearing.

"But he was always like this," Selena protested. "It is why I left in the first place." He didn't stand up for her after the shooting. He didn't stand up for her that day when a senior agent called her to his cubicle, swung his chair around, and patted his thighs, saying *Hey, dollface, have a seat. Whatzamatta? I thought Latin chicks were hot,* and she smacked him and he had her written up.

"*Luz de la calle, obscuridad de la casa,*" Comadre María quoted. Sometimes people do things in public they wouldn't dare do at home. She fingered the *tortillas* until they were perfectly round and the size of a large Host.

Selena waved her hands. "I'm not even sure why he needs me for this job," she fussed. *I'm on the list, sure, but that's no reason to pull me into the hunt — except I know La Serpiente well —* "There is nothing I can really add except, perhaps, my Spanish."

"*Al nopal solo lo van a ver cuando tiene tunas,*" Comadre María answered. People are interested in you when they can get something out of you. "Speaking of that, my child," she added with a grin, "start the *café de olla, por favor.*"

Selena opened the coffee tin and found the cinnamon. Was she just whining again, the way she did when cute Bobby Barszewski asked Gloria García to the Sweetheart Dance instead of her and she cried all the way here on the bus? What proverb had her *Madrina* offered then? Ah, yes: *No hay mal que por bien no venga.* There is nothing bad from which good does not come.

Comadre María tested the stove's heat with her palm and stirred the beans with a wooden spoon, adding a pinch of pepper. She dropped a tortilla into a pan, where it sizzled and browned. When it was ready, she slid it onto Selena's waiting plate. Selena swabbed butter on it and devoured it. She hadn't eaten since early morning. Her *Madrina* knew it somehow, again.

Selena took her usual chair, and her *Madrina* felt her way to the small drop-leaf table, where the old woman sat, crossed herself, and said grace. Selena recited it with her. Jesus, white as vanilla, watched them from the picture above them, touching his Sacred Heart. After the *amén,* Selena eagerly tore off pieces of tortilla to scoop up beans, something she loved to do as a kid out of her mother's critical sight. Afterward, she washed the dishes and put them away.

"You have been very quiet today, *pequeña hija*," her *Madrina* said. "Are you sure there isn't something else you wish to speak about?"

Selena hung up the tea towel and paused. She had always told her *Madrina* everything. "I am about to have a big change in my life, and I'm afraid, *Madrina*."

The woman raised her brows and offered an encouraging smile. "*Poco a poco se anda lejos*," she said. You can go far step by step.

"This will be a big step," Selena said.

"Ahh," the woman nodded knowingly. "Not the job. What is his name?"

She almost said it, and then thought better of it. "*Madrina*," Selena asked softly, "how do you know when you really love someone?"

"Come here, child. Give me your hands."

Selena returned to the table and sat down. She placed her hands in the woman's flour-smeared palms, lined with the many joys and trials of a long life.

"You know what I told you long ago," the woman said. "Do you remember?"

"*Más vale pájaro en mano que cien volando?*" A bird in the hand is worth more than one hundred flying away?

"No," she said with a little laugh. "Think. What did I tell you?"

"That I'll know I really love someone when I ask you that question?"

"That's right."

She gave Selena's hands an affectionate squeeze, held on, and waited.

Selena pressed her eyes shut. She couldn't tell her about Reed, if only because she would surely remind her of the time in high school she brought home an Anglo boy, Jerry, to meet the family. She feared *Papá* would interrogate him like a cop drilling a suspect, and the family, one by one, would corner him with stories of Mexico even if they couldn't speak English, and *Mamí* would serve tripe soup with *chiles colorados* to test his mettle — but she brought home the Anglo boy anyway. A crowd of *Mamí*, *Papá*, her three brothers, all her cousins, uncles and aunts, including Comadre María with all the curious, chattering neighbors greeted him. Jerry shook hands with *Papá* and her three brothers and smiled at everyone else — not knowing he was expected to meet everyone personally with a handshake and a warm verbal greeting. She should have told him. Later, *Mamí* called him *muy frío*, very cold, *mal educado*, ill mannered. *Is this how we raised you — to find a gringo for a boyfriend who is so bent on dishonoring us, who has no respeto for our familia?*

He doesn't know our ways, Selena cried. *He is Americano.*

And what are you? Mamí asked.

And Selena realized fully for the first time she was in two worlds at once.

Selena shuffled her feet, and Comadre María sighed. "Tell me more when you are ready, *querida*. You were raised in *las viejas costumbres*, the old ways, and I know you will choose *un caballero*, a good and polite man. There is no hurry." She released Selena's hands. "*Hasta la semana que entra, eh?* See you next week? For Thanksgiving, *sí?* Bring your friend if you like. To meet the *familia*."

She couldn't. And would there even *be* a next week? Selena arose and hugged the woman, kissing her on the ear. "*Gracias, Madrina. Te quiero mucho.*" I love you very much.

Comadre María could always see things she could not.

Even if she was blind.

CHAPTER 17

They don't move unless they're mating.

Or hunting.

And they hate to be moved.

Most of them like their steel-and-glass homes, the size of a shoebox or aquarium. But the barba amarilla needed a new cubicle now that he's seven feet — almost eight — from his triangular head down his dorsal line to the stony tail-tip. Nervous sucker. Lunged at me twice before I got a good hold on him with the tongs. Now I see why some people keep boas. They're slow and don't bite. Sure am glad for the gloves. Made them myself from rubber garden gloves, the kind with the nubby grippers.

Made this gizmo, too. It's not exactly like the shift box built onto the back of every cage with a sliding shutter for those times the darlings need to be moved to clean up. This one's got two doors. The second door is this bottom panel. That's why the whole thing is lifted up on this frame.

I punch these three numbers into my cell phone — boop, boop, beep — and it trips the latch from all the way across the room. The bottom drops open, and if the snake is in there, he drops to the floor and is mad about it. Wants to hurt somebody bad.

Better than Brinks or any other home security system, I say.

And pity the poor person who might be locked inside the greenhouse, alone in the dark with, let's say, not even the moon for a light.

CHAPTER 18

After Thanksgiving dinner, the men sprawled on the plastic-covered chairs in *Comadre* María's living room, swigging beers and yelling at *fútbol* on TV while the women chattered loudly over the stove and sink in the *cocina*. Handing each other plastic containers, they were putting away the leftovers of traditional American fare — turkey, celery and cornbread stuffing, mashed garlic potatoes, green-bean casserole with onions, corn with red bell peppers, yams with marshmallow, and cranberry relish. *Papá* had always insisted that his children fit in and be acculturated, but not assimilated. Selena couldn't help but smile at the fact that all the traditional "American" foods were indigenous to Mexico, except for the cranberry.

Lorenzo's two kids pulled out a *Serpientes y Escaleras* board game on the parlor floor and argued about who should go first.

"Hey, none of that!" Lorenzo barked. "*Los niños hablan cuando las gallinas mean.*"

Selena and her brothers had heard it often: *Children speak when hens pee.* And everyone knows, *pues claro*, hens don't pee.

"The chipotle and chive cornbread was yours, wasn't it, Selena, dear?" asked Auntie Big Hair, who was stuffed into a satin dress two sizes too small for her.

"*Sí*, that was mine," Selena said. "New recipe." She got it from *Latina* magazine.

"*Delish-io-sho*," Auntie said, mouth full. She licked her fingers and glossy nails. "At last you are learning to cook. Why aren't you cooking for a man yet? *¿Cuando te vas a casar?* When are you going to settle down?"

"I'm trying to establish my business," Selena said.

"What would your mother say?" Auntie Big Hair said. "Do you want to end up like *la Cucarachita Martina*?"

It was a familiar fairy tale — the little girl cockroach Martina finds a nickel and, after much thought, uses it to buy powder to look pretty and find a husband. She refuses the proposals of the dog, the cat, and the rooster because they bark, hiss, and crow, *"Aqui mando yo,"* *I give the orders here,* when asked what they will do on their wedding night. Finally Perez the mouse wins her *amor* by his caring and gentle demeanor, because *Latinas* at heart desire a gentleman like that. But as *Cucarachita Martina* is making a stew for the wedding feast like a good wife and *una buena mujer* should, Perez gets impatient, and while trying to taste it, he falls into the pot and drowns. Lesson: *el destino* will take you away from the good man you hoped for and you'll have to settle for a man driven by *machismo.*

Auntie Giggles bare-shouldered her way into the conversation, floral taffeta swishing. "What's this I hear? Hee-hee! Selena is going to settle down? You found a man at last? *¡Que milagro!"*

"It's — it's not like that," Selena struggled.

"So there *is* someone," Auntie Big Hair gushed. "Who is it? Tell me. Does he have a car as nice as yours?"

"I'm not seeing anyone right now," Selena said, wishing that Reed, chivalrous, chisel-chinned, and smart, were here to take the pressure off her.

Auntie Giggles pouted. *"¿Qué pasa?* A curvy *chica* like you still *sola?"*

Selena firmed her lips. Every *Latina* knew that an unmarried and childless woman hasn't lived up to the expectations of the *familia.*

"I guess I want *Señor* Right, not *Señor* Right Now," she said. It was a ragged cliché, but it might stop the women's badgering.

Her brother Lorenzo belched wetly and called out for more black-bean dip. His wife, Elena, scooped some from a plastic bowl into a decorative dish.

"And another beer!" Francisco hollered. Then a player muffed a kick, and both brothers stood with Uncle Hairy Nose and Uncle Baldy and three cousins to shake their fists and shout insults at the TV.

Elena grabbed four beer bottles from the fridge and closed the door with her knee.

"They're big boys, Elena," Selena said. "They can get their rumps up and get their own beers."

"I'd answer for it later," she said quietly. "Excuse me."

"Hey, that's not the one I want," Lorenzo complained. "The Corona Light. And put a little wedge of lime in it, OK?"

Francisco shook the chip basket. "We need more chips, too. Those blue ones."

Elena set down the dip. "Sure. Right away, *mi vida*."

Selena crossed her arms. "My brother is a lazy slob," she told Elena when she re-entered the kitchen. "You're encouraging him. Make him get up now and then. Why serve him hand and foot?"

"Your *Mamí* did," she said, brushing past her. "All Mexican mothers do. You know that. Or maybe not."

Comadre María asked Selena to step aside so she could wipe the countertop.

"Oh, let me do it for you," Selena offered, uneasy about Elena's snippy remark.

"No, no. I'm fine," *Madrina* said. "You relax and enjoy. There's plenty left over. Take some home." She squeezed Selena's arm. "Still so skinny. Take it all home. If only you weren't so far away. Why be so far away? You have to drive all that way in that old car. And it sounds worse than the last time you were here. Maybe you can have the *mecánico de auto* look at it before you leave."

Selena smiled. How could she explain that it was *supposed* to be loud? "*Madrina*, it is best for everyone that I live where I am right now."

"Your mother felt the same way as me. Why so far? Living alone in that big house? How can your brothers protect you when you are so far from the *familia*? We just want you to be safe."

Lorenzo belched again, and Francisco laughed like a *burro*.

"It is best for all of us that I am far away," Selena repeated.

CHAPTER 19

Bragg told Selena that there was no need to wear a wire. The house was wired.

The framed living-room mirror was a two-way with a tripod-mounted digital camera behind it, taped up to hide its instrument lights. Bragg and four of his finest crouched behind the mirror, sweating in their body armor, semiautomatics ready, earpieces abuzz. The delivery truck across the street was a studio and stake-out command center, relaying information about street traffic. Unmarked cars lurked around the corners. Bragg's plan: Once The Snake arrived and was trapped inside, the men moved in, sealing all exits. Bragg would tackle him before he could reach a firearm.

Miguel sat on a vinyl couch, knees apart, bent forward and cleaning his fingernails with a pocketknife. "So what's up with the shoes?" he asked.

"What about them?" Selena sat up in the chair and slipped her heel out of her plum-and-lemon pump. "Don't like the colors?"

"I mean, like, *chicas* dig shoes, but these — these must cost a lot."

"Dolce and Gabbanas. Courtesy of the dealers we bust," she said. "Seized money pays for a lot of our equipment. This is my equipment. Technically, these belong to the agency." She swung her heel. "You'd be surprised. They don't cost as much as the parts for my car."

"Yeah? You fix your own car?"

She wiggled her fingers. "It's why the nails are short."

"Whaddya got?"

" '69 Dodge Charger. 440 Magnum V8, 450 horse. A two-barrel Carter carburetor I rebuilt. I fabbed the exhaust system myself."

He whistled. "Sweet. What color?"

"Chili Pepper Red. What else?"

"*¿Uno carro caliente, eh?*"

"*Sí,* very nice."

"So, you drag with it?"

"I just drive it to church on Sundays."

"Yeah, right," he snorted. "So what's it do?"

"Zero to 60 in 3-point-9. But I stick to the speed limit. Got enough tickets as a teenager to last my whole life."

He tapped his chest and grunted. "Yeah, me too."

She consulted the wall clock. 4:50. "You told him five o'clock, right?"

"Don't worry; he won't be late," he said. "He knew it was you right away when I told him about the shoes. Does he know about your boyfriend?"

"What?"

"Bragg tells me you're sweet on a *gringo.* So you marryin' out of *la raza* or what?

"No," she said curtly. She bristled at the hint she was betraying her race but more than that, angered at being betrayed by Bragg. *What right does he have to tell a CI about my private life? The nerve.* She drew a long breath to calm herself. "Tell me: Did The Snake pay you to keep me here? To make sure I don't leave early?"

"What do you think?"

"I think you're enjoying this. Playing both sides. That's what you're doing, isn't it?"

"It beats landscaping or bussing tables."

Bragg knocked at the mirror twice. Tik, tik. Someone was coming.

"Showtime," Selena said, sliding into the shoe and rising. She smoothed her Lady Pendleton slacks. She told her heart to slow down. She tugged a hoop earring and cupped her ear, listening. "You weren't expecting anyone else, were you?"

"Not this early." He snapped the knife closed and crammed it into his cargo-pants pocket.

Muffled laughter filtered through the front door, feet stomped, and a thump sounded on the door.

"*¡Oye ese! ¿Que hay de nuevo*, huh?" called a drunken voice.

"*Caray*," Miguel said, smacking his forehead, "it's my *carnales*. I'll get rid of them *pronto*."

Loud knocking. *Bam bam.* "*¿Qué onda, güey*, you in there or what?" the voice called from outside. *Bam bam.*

"*¡Cállate la boca!* Shut up!" Miguel yelled. He hustled to the door and threw it open.

Three young men tumbled in, stinking of stale beer. Their pants were low, their spirits as high as crystal meth could take them, caps cocked, sport parkas open, hands gesturing.

One clapped Miguel on the shoulder. "Sup, dawg, we gonna get *pistiao* tonight or what?"

The fat boy behind him belched. "*Oye*, I had a few *cheves* already, and I'm all messed up."

The third, in a hoodie and vest, jerked his thumb to the street. "I got the *yesca* and beer, Miguel, you got the *pisto* here?"

He angled his head and caught sight of Selena.

"Whoo-eee," he exclaimed with a clap. "*Está bueniiiisima*, eh? Dudes, we're, like, interruptin' something here."

One of them wolf-whistled.

Selena glared at them. "*Hierba mala nunca muere*," she said. Bad weed never dies.

"It's just business," Miguel said, jittery. "*Luego hablamos*, ok? Your place. Maybe in an hour."

"Oh, it's that kind of business, huh? Think you'll last a whole hour? You need different drugs for that," the boy snickered. He winked and elbowed Miguel, lowering his voice. "You got a good *mango de manila* this time, *güey*. Isn't she a little old for you, though?"

"Get out," Miguel said, spinning him and pushing him from behind. "I'll bring some good *perico* to your crib later, huh? We'll get stinkin' *grifo*, OK? I promise."

The boy wagged a finger at him. "The last stuff was good," he agreed. "C'mon, dudes. *Vámonos*."

"Hey, what's your name, baby?" the fat one called over his shoulder, sniggering.

Selena planted her palm on her hip. "*La Bruja*," she breathed.

They paled, their laughter stopped and they tripped over themselves down the steps, fell into their beat-up Escort, and with a screech, pulled away.

"Did you have to say that?" Miguel asked.

"It's true," she replied.

"The Witch?"

"Just ask Bragg. He'll tell you so."

"Sheesh, did you have to give them the evil eye, too?"

"All they have to do is put a poached egg under their bed tonight and no harm done, *sí*?"

Miguel leaned out the open door to make sure they were gone. "*Cucarachas*," he muttered.

Bragg stormed into the room, his face red as hot *chilis*. He waved his Glock carelessly. "What was that all about? I thought you said you had no other appointments."

Miguel pivoted. "Hey, it's just my boys —"

A truck blared its horn twice in the street.

Bragg poked the boy in the chest and barked in his face. "Or maybe they're scouts, huh? Did you think of that? Did you? I almost busted in here to take them down. It would have screwed up the whole thing."

"They're gone, ok? Chill, man."

Another man from the camera room raced in. "They're here."

The two-horn blast. The signal.

A figure filled the open doorway, cursed, and spun away.

"*¡La policía!*" he cried.

Bragg dashed to the door, swearing. Another man outside leaped into a waiting Chevy Blazer beside the driver, urging the third on. "*¡Córrele!* Hurry up!"

Bragg lifted his weapon. "Stop! On your knees! Or I'll shoot!"

Officers from the delivery truck spilled out, pistols raised. "Out of the car! Now!" they shouted. "*¡Muestren las manos!* Show your hands!"

The driver revved the engine. The passenger drew a pistol and took aim.

Bragg fired. Again. Again. Again.

The bullets struck the running man and the Blazer beyond him. Safety glass splintered. The running man dropped like a flour sack and was still. Officers rushed the vehicle, ripped open the doors, and dragged out the driver and the passenger. They threw the shooter to the pavement and kicked away his gun. They slammed the driver across the hood, kicked his legs apart and rifled his pockets. Someone began reading their rights in Spanish, reading from a phonetic cue card.

Bragg approached the man on the ground, gripping his tactical Glock 35 pistol with two hands, the barrel raised and centered on the prone body the whole time. Selena ran alongside him, breathing hard, tugging her brown bombardier jacket closed.

"Is he dead?" she asked.

"Looks it," Bragg said bluntly.

"Is it him?"

"Let's see." He lodged his boot toe under the body and rolled it over. The face belonged to a young gang banger — wispy beard below the lip, a nose ring, tattoos on his hands.

"Recognize him at all?" Bragg asked Selena.

She leaned forward. Pressed her palms on her knees. Turned away from the blank, surprised eyes. Fought off the nausea at the sound of gurgling and the stink of intestinal gas. "Gonzalez," she said, her throat as dry as wool. "It's Eddie Gonzalez. They called him 'Speedy Gonzalez' for the speed he sold to kids in Little Mexico."

"Yeah, well, it wasn't because he could run fast."

"You didn't have to shoot him," Selena said. "He obviously wasn't armed."

"Nothing's ever obvious, except that the other guy certainly *was* armed. This guy got in the way." Bragg stood tall, shaded his eyes, and scanned the other two men being cuffed and stuffed into cruisers. "Neither one of those guys is our man. You know them?"

Selena shook her head.

"Well, let's go introduce ourselves at the station," Bragg said, "while the boys secure the scene for the techies."

Selena brushed her hair back. Something was wrong. Why was Eddie here instead of The Snake, as Miguel promised? Did The Snake smell something and send Eddie in his place as a scout?

Miguel stood in the doorway. "Was that him?" he called.

"No," Bragg said. "Have a look and tell us if you know him."

"Geez, do I have to?"

"Get over here," Bragg ordered.

Miguel sauntered near, leaned forward and spun away, a hand over his mouth. "No," he said with a gag. "Never seen him."

"You sure? Take another look."

"Yeah, I'm sure. I don't need another look."

"How about those two guys across the street?"

Miguel watched them getting cuffed. "Nope."

"We'll see what IDs they had and run their prints," Bragg said. "We'll trace the gun's registration, too, and find out who owns the Blazer. I'm betting it's stolen." He secured his sidearm and squinted at the body by his feet. "We gotta call the M.E., and I'll have a pile of paperwork because of this," he grumbled. "Gonzalez, you said?"

Selena nodded. "Eddie."

"Like in Eduardo?"

"No. Edgar."

Bragg scratched his head. "You know something?" he said. "That sounds familiar."

"I know. He used to work for The Snake."

"No, not that. Did he have any aliases?"

"Let's see: Ned Costa, Eddie Castro."

As soon as she said it, her heart climbed into her throat.

"Say," Bragg said, tapping his chin, "isn't that the name two spaces before you on the list?"

Her teeth clenched. "Yes."

"Ain't it strange?" Bragg kicked the corpse. "Looks like we saved The Snake some trouble, Selena. You know what this means, don't you?"

Her heart raced. "One more. Then me."

CHAPTER 20

Selena swept her cheeks and brow bones with a ginger blush and re-freshed the Sandpiper lipstick, rubbing her lips together and then puffing them at the ladies' room mirror. She turned left and right, unhappy as always with the sundial of a nose her Zapotec ancestors had bequeathed to her. Nothing to be done about that. She brushed out her hair big. It was time to be *Latina*, not *Angla*, she decided, touching up with raven eye pencil. The *hombres* in Interview Rooms One and Two expected a tough cop, but a curvy *chica* in killer shoes might surprise them and open them up. She tugged her blouse tighter, fluffed the collar, adjusted her tapered jacket, and returned to the squad room, clicking across the tiles in her plum Dolce and Gabbanas with the lemon stripes. Bragg wolf-whistled as he handed her a fistful of beige manila folders.

"Hey, I thought you were helping with the interview, not doing undercover with vice," he said.

"Just tell me who we've got here, Del," she said, opening the top folder.

"Julio Vasquez and Roberto De Jesus — if those are their real names on the Social Security cards," Bragg said skeptically. "Funny that they should be carrying them, don'tcha think? I mean, like, who does?"

"Day laborers," Selena noted, studying the photos. "I presume you're checking the numbers?"

"Gordon's on it."

"Any other ID?"

"Roberto, the younger guy driving the vehicle, has a legit driver's license. This one here, Julio, the one who tried to shoot me, has some video-store membership cards and that's it."

She flipped through the arrest report. "What have they said so far?"

Bragg guffawed. "Not much. Their English is as good as my Spanish."

"That's not saying much. So you want me to interpret for you?"

"Nah. You go ahead and ask the questions, Selena. I'll stand by and be the bad cop."

It was a role he enjoyed.

"Didn't they say anything at all yet, Del?"

"All they'll tell us is the name of their most recent employer, River Falls Rendering. It's a sausage factory that works with hog operations year-round and deer hunters in fall. Bet they're busy now. Gordon's men are calling them, and we'll contact ICE later to see if they know them."

At least they hadn't asked for a lawyer. Selena thumbed the pages. "No priors, I see. That's unusual. Have you run the prints with AFIS already?"

"Yeah. Nothing so far."

"What do we know about the gun?"

"Unregistered Beretta. We're tracking the serial number — what isn't filed off — to find the seller if we can."

"Any cell phones?"

"Yeah, one. Julio's. We'll check the numbers in the address book. For Eddie's phone, too. I've requested a warrant for the cell phone records. We should get them in just a couple hours."

"What do we know about the car?" Selena asked.

"Stolen. Like I guessed. It was reported yesterday. After the evidence team is through with it, we'll contact the owner."

"Hope he's got good insurance. Maybe I'll call him and see if he'll switch carriers," Selena said with a wry wrinkle of her nose. "OK then, let's see if either of these two have met The Snake through Eddie and will turn into an informant and lead us to our man. Got the mug shots?"

"Green folder."

She opened it. The glossy photo lineup pictured six unidentified men. Top row, third from the left: The Snake. His glassy black eyes met hers, sending a chill to the small of her back, where his fingernails had dug into her that one time they danced. She snapped the folder shut. "One more thing," she said. "Do we have a mug of the other vic, the man in the cemetery?"

"Sure. A bunch. How gross you want them?"

"Just the face." She slapped the folder against Bragg's chest. "If we say we suspect them of murder — especially that one — they might open up."

"Gotcha. Wait here a minute."

Bragg approached the desk sergeant, spoke to him, and the man opened a file drawer.

The suspects in Interview Rooms One and Two probably had nothing to do with the cemetery murder or the others like it, Selena surmised. It was the work of a single, organized killer working by a plan according to the Book of the Deceased. The missing organs bothered her. It wasn't like The Snake to be ritualistic, cleaning up and leaving a signature flower. He was your basic thug, an opportunist. She'd ask them anyway. Surely they'd heard of it and might even fear being the next victim announced by The Blue Lady. And with the feast day of Our Lady of Guadalupe coming up, the emotions would be running high in the *barrios*, especially if Jacinta had any more visions in which she —

"Ready?" Bragg asked, snapping his fingers in her face. He didn't wait for an answer. He bustled past her down the hall to the observation room between Interview Rooms One and Two. The door was labeled *storage*. Selena stepped in, inspecting the small two-way windows on either side. In each cinderblock room, the mirror hung over a steel sink as a way to disguise its true nature. Each detainee sat slumped alone in hard straight-back chairs. Julio, the older man, fidgeted and bit his lip. He had something to hide. Roberto, the younger man at the wheel, sat still and hard as a stone. He was plain scared.

A uniformed officer at the recording console rose to greet Selena. He looked fresh from the Academy, rosy-cheeked and toothy. Rural districts often got the newbies. "Roy B-Blanchard, ma'am," he said. "Detective Gordon here told me all about your work."

"Really? You know, my agency is running an introductory special on Term Life policies," she said with a smile. "Come see me."

"Not that work," Gordon said, looking up from a clipboard. "Do you want to start with Julio, the shooter? He looks pretty nervous."

"Let's start with the boy Roberto. He's scared and more likely to cooperate. We have him on possible immigration problems, and that's about all."

Bragg huffed. "He was in a stolen car during a drug run and an accessory to an assault on a police officer with a deadly weapon. Isn't that enough?"

"He might have been along for the ride," Selena said. "Look at him. He's shaking."

"He's just not used to winter in Illinois, that's all," Bragg said.

"I'm not, and I was raised here," Selena said. "Say, have we searched the residence listed on the license yet?"

"Just got the warrant," Gordon said. "Our guys are there now."

"Are we recording, Officer Blanchard?" Selena asked.

"Yes, ma'am." To demonstrate, Blanchard pushed up the console fader for the mic in Roberto's room. The chair scraped, and the boy sniffed.

Selena tugged her jacket smooth, hugged the folders, and stepped around to Interview Room One. "After you, Del," she said. Bragg burst in as though he was raiding the place.

Roberto, wide-eyed, sat up with a start. He folded his hands on top of the table. Red marks of the zip-ties still showed on his wrists. His fingernails were ragged and stained from smoking. His wavy black hair, smelling of *Tres Flores* oil, was as shiny as Selena's shoes.

Bragg circled behind the adolescent and shouldered against the wall the way he liked to do, arms crossed.

Selena sat opposite the young Latino. She set the folders in front of her. She observed his eyes widening to see a woman in a business suit and heels.

"*No soy una mujer policía,*" she said calmly to the young man. I'm not a policewoman.

Puzzlement replaced the look of surprise. "*¿Qué entonces? ¿Abogado?*" What, then — a lawyer?

"No."

"*¿La Migra?* Immigration?"

"No."

"Then why are you here, *agringada?*"

She brushed aside the rude slight, like calling someone black an Oreo. "*Ay,* the *gringos* in these small towns. They can't speak *Español,* so they bring me in," she explained with a little roll of her eyes.

"I don't believe it. You just want me to say something to you that I wouldn't say to him," he said. "I bet he speaks *Español* real good."

She shrugged. "Go ahead. Say something insulting to him. But look at me when you say it. You'll see."

He smirked. He made a rude comment about Bragg's manhood. Bragg didn't budge.

"See?" Selena said. "No reaction from *el cochino.*" And he really was a pig. "Even I can say that."

He laughed.

"What's so funny?" Bragg asked.

"My shoes," Selena said.

Bragg snorted. "He hasn't seen your weirdest ones."

She leaned toward the man. "*Escúchame,* Roberto, listen up good: level with me, and I'll get you out of here. This guy is no regular cop. He's Drug Enforcement, a *federal,* and he wants to beat you like a *piñata* until your insides spill out."

"Who are you really?"

"An insurance agent."

"*¿A poco?*" Really?

"Look me up after this. I'll check your coverage — if you have any. Your car looks awful, you know. All those busted windows, the holes —"

"It's not my car."

"Whose is it?"

"I dunno. Eddie's, I guess."

"Wrong. It's a stolen car. The crime is called grand theft auto here in *el norte,* and it will put your sorry butt in jail for a very long time."

He blanched. "I didn't know it was stolen. How could I know that?"

"I'll tell you what I know, Roberto. Look at me. Based on what I've heard from Julio, you knew that it was stolen and that you were using the car for a drug run with Eddie."

"He's a liar!"

Guilty ones usually delayed, changed posture, crossed their arms, considered their reply. The innocent ones shot back like this. A good start.

She rapped her blunt fingernails on the tabletop. "You know what? I want to believe you. I really do. But for now, I need to get beyond the fact you were in a stolen car at a drug house, where your partner aimed a gun at a policeman —"

"I didn't know where we were going! I didn't know he had a gun!"

"Listen to me. Are you listening? There are two sides to every story, ¿no? And all I have now is one side. I need your side so I can get the truth working for you instead of against you. I'm not trying to put the blame on you. *Ay,* if you hadn't gotten mixed up with Julio and those other guys, you wouldn't have gone to a *picadero,* a drug house, right? It wasn't your idea."

"I didn't know —"

"Let me finish. Here is the problem. You were in the car. You were the driver. So even if you didn't kill anybody or hurt anybody, you drove them there." She shook her head with a hint of disappointment.

"That's what is called an accessory. It's not fair, but there you are. The *gringo* cop behind you is going to lump you together with Julio and Eddie and whoever else Eddie was hanging out with. You know who I mean."

"I'm telling you, I didn't do —"

"We're past that, Roberto. It's no longer a question if you did it. You were there. You were driving the car. Now it's about where we go from here. Are you listening, Roberto? Lift up your head. If you help me, maybe I can help you. I need you to look at some pictures for me, OK? These *fotografías*."

She opened the top folder and spun around the shiny photos.

"Do you recognize any of these men, Roberto? Did any of them ever visit with you or Julio? Did you ever see Eddie with any one of them?"

Roberto picked up the print. His hand trembled a little. He tilted his head as though it would give him a better look. He sniffed and spun away the page.

"I don't know any of them."

"Are you sure, Roberto? Here, look again."

He gave the paper a perfunctory glance, licked his lips, and said, "No."

Bragg lurched forward, seized the boy's arm, and jerked him up. "Listen, you dumb beaner, listen good because if you don't tell us the truth, I'm gonna put you through the meat grinder at your sausage factory."

"*¡Yo no sé nada!*" he shrieked, tears spurting. "Not a thing!"

Bragg pulled back a fist. "Let me knock it out of him!"

"What do you want?" Roberto cried.

"Del, let him go," Selena said.

Bragg released him. Roberto dropped into the seat. He rubbed his arm.

Selena leaned forward. "Roberto, as I said, I know you didn't plan to go to a drug house. If you did, I wouldn't be spending time with you right now. But that's not all that happened, right? What happened before you got in the car with Eddie and Julio? How was the decision made?"

"Eddie, he says he wants to run an errand quick and asks me to drive."

"Why not himself?"

"License got suspended."

Something else to track down — when, where, for what reason. "What was the errand?"

"*Ibamos de compras*," he said.

"Just to buy groceries?"

"*Sí*. Eddie says he's got a grocery errand to run and we get our coats and get in the car and Eddie gives me the keys and he says where to go. And then we pull up to this house and Eddie says he'll be a minute and to keep the car running. And then, when he gets to the door, he shouts out and runs for it and is shot by that *gringo* behind me. The windows, they break up. I see Julio pull out this gun from his coat and there's, like, bullets flying. And then police pull me into the street. They yell at me. That's all."

He was breathing hard.

"OK, Roberto, *gracias*, that's helpful. This is hard for you, eh? Not been in the country long, I take it? You have family here?"

He shook his head.

"Just a grocery errand, huh?" she said.

"*Sí*, groceries."

"Did Eddie say why he was stopping at this house on the way?"

"No."

"Did he say he was being sent there by someone else?"

"No."

Selena observed him for a moment. His eyes shifted. She waited.

"OK, that's it." She slid the chair back. Checked her watch. "I'm telling the *gringo* here you're not being cooperative anymore and I can go back to my office. I've got work to do."

"No, no, wait a minute, just a minute," he said.

"Memory coming back to you? Tell me what happened. Tell me the truth, and I'll tell the *gringo* cop to go easy on you. That you didn't know what was happening. OK? Start before you left the house."

He fingered his collar. "Eddie, I dunno — after this phone call on his cell, he says there's this house where there's good stuff, better'n he's got, that he can resell later, you know?"

"Who made the phone call?"

"Eddie didn't say."

"What time was the call?"

"I forget. No, around noon. Yeah, noon."

"You're sure? OK, that's good. I have one more question for you."

She opened the folder with the photo of the cemetery victim. She held up the photo at eye level. "Do you recognize this man, Roberto?"

The young man averted his eyes and crossed himself. "*Ten misericordia de mí, Madrecita,*" he said with a gulp.

"So you know him?" Selena asked.

"Who doesn't?" Roberto said. "He is the one Our Lady said would die. She left her flowers on him, a sign."

"How do you know that?"

"Everyone knows that."

"Why would she do such a harsh thing, Roberto? Our Holy Mother — our life, our sweetness, and our hope?"

"She is angry. Her Son is angry." He shuddered and wiped his eyes. "That girl who sees her — she says so."

"Jacinta?"

"*Sí,* that one. The Lady tells her to say so in the streets after every visit, that she and her son are angry with those who harm her people."

"Do you know why they are angry, Roberto? I'll tell you. It is because of gangs like yours that bring shame on our people. It is because of men like you who sell drugs to our young *chamacos*. Look at the picture, Roberto. Would you like to be next? Or would you like to show Our Lady you are ready to repent? You can, by promising to help us."

"I — It is —" He sniffled.

"You stay here and pray about it," Selena said. "Because if you ask me, I think you are going to be next."

She levered up and tucked the folders under her arm. "We're done here, Del," she said and went out, heels clicking.

CHAPTER 21

"I think he was kept in the dark about it," she said in the hall. "But I think he'll help us. Let's see what Julio knew."

She stepped into the recording room on the way. "Have you heard any news from your search team?" she asked Gordon.

Gordon raised his arms in a touchdown sign. "Weed, scales, baggies, pipes, all kinds of stuff, and fingerprints galore. These guys are toast."

"Anything from the phone company yet?"

"We're lucky. Slow day at court. We got the warrant right away. I'm expecting a fax any minute. Then we'll find out who called Eddie at noon," Gordon said.

"Interrupt us if there's news," she said. "Let's go, Del."

She stepped to the door of Interview Two, took a breath, and opened the door. She bustled in, all business, and smacked the folders on the table.

Julio Vasquez jerked his rheumy eyes up at her. He laughed. "*Yo no voy a hablar con una mujer,*" he growled, showing his cracked teeth. I'm not going to talk to a woman.

Selena didn't bother to sit. She planted her palms on the edge of the table and leaned forward, ignoring the man's smell. "*Si eso es lo que quieres, pues bien,* really, perfectly fine with me," she said evenly. "Since you're here on a charge of assaulting a federal officer with intent to kill, we'll assign your case to Homeland Security and have you rendered to Guantanamo for questioning there. You'll find the weather in Cuba more agreeable."

"Guantanamo?" he said, eyes squinted in disbelief. "That's for *terroristas.*"

"Haven't you heard? They're closing it down for terrorists but keeping it open for *narcotraficantes,* even small traffickers like you," Selena replied. "I'll enjoy watching the tapes they send back to us."

"Hey," Julio objected, "all I did was —"

"All you did was what, Julio? Draw a loaded weapon to fire at Officer Bragg here? Your prints are all over it. Several officers saw it was you and will say so in court. You'll get twenty years, Julio."

"All they'll do is deport me," he sneered.

"To Cuba," she said.

"You're not serious."

"Dead serious."

He raked his black hair straight back. "What do you want?" he asked.

Selena sat. Folded her hands. "I want to know who called you and Eddie on the phone just before you left for the drug house."

"That's all?"

"That's all."

"Then you'll let me go?"

"Then I'll tell this *gringo* cop you are cooperating, and we'll cancel your flight to Cuba."

He stared into her eyes. She didn't flinch. All those poker games with her brothers.

"Eddie said it was a big dealer he knew. A chance to get back in the business. Even be a partner with this guy if Eddie proved himself one more time."

"That's what the caller said?"

"*Sí.*"

"And the caller's name?"

"He didn't give a name."

"No deal."

Julio wet his lips. "OK. He only said it was a man who calls himself *La Serpiente*."

Bragg straightened up. He knew that word. "It was him?" he asked.

"You're sure?" Selena pressed, heart pounding. "*La Serpiente?* The Snake?"

"That's what Eddie said."

Selena opened the folder with the mug-shot sheet. She slid it across the table. "Recognize anyone here?"

"Why should I?"

"Have a look."

Julio traced the thumbnails with a finger stained by nicotine. He shook his head. "Who are these men?"

"Some local dealers we know about," Selena said. "Did any of them come to the house you and Roberto and Eddie were in?"

He frumped. "No. I have never seen them. Is one of them this Snake?"

"You tell me."

He crossed his arms. "I'm not telling you any more."

"That's it," Bragg growled, planting his hand on Julio's neck and shoving his face close to the pictures. "Take a gooood look again, buster," he said. "Is this the guy? This one right here?" He stabbed a finger on the photo of The Snake.

Julio tried to wriggle away from Bragg's grip. Bragg pushed his nose to the page.

Selena said, "*El policía* wants to know if you have seen this man."

"I told you," Julio puffed, nose crushed against the tabletop, "I do not know any of them."

"Greasy liar," Bragg snarled. "I want the truth. El trutho."

"*La verdad*, Julio," Selena translated.

Bragg released him roughly.

"I have told you the truth. Do I get a lawyer now?" Julio asked.

"It's too late for that," Selena said. Good thing he didn't actually ask for one. "We'll talk again later. You have been helpful, and we will remember it." She left the room, Bragg close behind.

"Nailed that one," he said.

"No, Del, we didn't," Selena breathed.

"Why not?" he said, raising his hands. "He said it was The Snake who called, and he basically sent Eddie into the trap to check it out. All we have to do is trace the call, and we've got him. Every phone leaves a trail. Even out here in the country, we can track the signals to masts and triangulate to within a hundred yards. We assemble a tactical team and take him into custody."

Selena shook her head. "Call it woman's intuition. He wasn't lying. But he wasn't telling us the whole story, either."

Gordon emerged from the recording room waving a fax. "The phone company just sent a record of calls to Eddie's phone. There was a call at 12:06 from this number and this location." He pointed to it.

Selena asked, "Whose number is it?"

"It's assigned to a Carlos Ventura."

"Must be a fake ID," Bragg said. "Can they pinpoint where the call was made from?"

Gordon nodded. "Buffalo Grove, west side."

"That's where our drug house is." Bragg scratched his chin, perplexed.

"Well, Miguel said he knew where The Snake was," Selena said. "He was, as it may turn out, right in the neighborhood, waiting for the shooting to go down. Heck, he may have been near enough to observe it."

"Let's call the number right now," Bragg said. "Maybe The Snake will answer and we can run a trace."

Gordon handed her the phone ceremoniously. "Be my guest. I'll get on the horn with the phone company and have them stand by to pinpoint the location for us."

Selena took the phone, flipped it open, and gripped it so tightly, she worried that it might break. What was she supposed to say? *Hola, amigo, es Selena. Long time no see, ¿no? How've ya been? That bust wasn't my fault, you know. It had to be a snitch on your side of things. Anyway, I gave The Barracuda to the Feds so they let me go. We should get together. Pick up where we left off, eh? Care to dance?*

"They're ready," Gordon announced.

Selena thumbed the numbers, stood erect, and collected herself. Why was her back tingling? Why was her throat suddenly dry?

Bee-dee-deee. The number you have reached is out of service. If you feel you have reached this number in error, please hang up and try again. The number you have reached is out of —

Selena snapped it shut. "Out of service. Not surprised."

"So now what?" Bragg wondered aloud. "Besides the fact that we hold onto these two *banditos*?"

He seemed proud about using a Spanish word, even if was a derogatory one and he didn't even pronounce it correctly.

"I'll go to Eddie's funeral tomorrow," Selena announced. "By custom, Mexicans bury their dead within 24 hours. And you know how killers sometimes show up to admire their work. *La Serpiente* might decide to pay his respects."

"What time is the funeral?" Bragg asked.

"Sorry," Selena said with a *no-way* wag of her head. "You guys had better not come. I'll blend in, but the *Mexicanos* will spot you a mile away and the word would get around fast. Even if I'm recognized, the locals know me as a harmless insurance agent. It wouldn't be at all unusual for me to be there. They'll figure I'm attending because it's good for business. I'll take the company Jeep with the Town and Country logo on the door."

"You'll need backup," Gordon objected. "We could park around the corner, even blocks away with phones —"

"No," Selena said bluntly. "No offense, but they'll smell you. Look, if I see something, I'll call."

"I don't like it," Gordon said. "You guys must have an Hispanic agent you can call in from Chicago."

"Well, there's Rudy Rodríguez," Bragg said.

Selena frowned. Rudy *what's-she-doing-here-this-is-a-man's-job* Rodríguez.

"Selena's right. It's undercover surveillance, and she needs to do it solo." Bragg brushed his beefy hands. "I couldn't come anyway, Selena," he declared. "Chicago Inspector's office called just before you arrived. I'm on suspension starting tomorrow, pending the internal review of the shooting. Routine."

He grinned.

"You know how that goes, don't you?" he said.

"Bless me, Father, for I have sinned," Selena had said that awful night, crossing herself quickly, chin on her chest. "It's been — oh, God. Sorry. It's been —"

"Don't worry about it," the shadowed priest whispered from behind the screen. "What's on your mind?"

"Father, I shot a little girl. She's in the hospital right now. They say she'll live."

"Shot her? An accident at home?"

"No, Father. I'm a Special Agent with the DEA. I was in a tactical squad raiding a home where the intel said there was a big meth operation, and I didn't agree and — well, I — I thought — I mean — it was dark, and I — I'm sorry."

"Take your time. Do you need a tissue?"

"No. I've got one." Selena fished a hanky from a pocket and dabbed at her nose.

"Would you rather sit and talk in the rectory?"

"No, Father," Selena said with a sniff. "This works for me. The guilt is killing me. I can't even see her to say how sorry I am. I'm not family. Hospital and Agency rules."

"Tell me what happened."

"OK. So we were searching the house. I was in the rear. I had my sidearm drawn, finger on the locator — you know, not on the trigger, alongside it, like we're trained to do. The squad leader called a room 'clear,' and the men continued to the next room, but I wasn't convinced. The TV set was warm, and it looked like someone had just jumped off the bed. The closet door was ajar. I yanked it open and — well, it looked like whoever was squatting in there was aiming a gun at my face so I — I didn't think. I just reacted. Startle response. I fired. God, it was just the remote control. That's all it was. A frightened little girl with a remote control."

"Daughter, I can tell this was traumatic for you. But in God's eyes, you didn't sin. You did your duty and followed your training."

"You mean well, Father, but I don't believe it. What if I had killed her? It wouldn't have been self-defense. It was a remote control, not a gun."

"But you *didn't* kill her. God was merciful to you both then. He is merciful now and surely will not judge you for an honest error. What you need isn't forgiveness, but fortitude. You needn't feel guilt, but instead gratitude that God in his grace preserved you both."

"I just wish others could be forgiving, Father," Selena said, sniffling. "You should hear what the men are saying. And I'm on automatic suspension, pending an investigation. It's the normal policy but — there was a TV crew there, recording for some cable show. Once that's out and once the press gets wind of this, they'll have my head."

"We can't know that for sure. Maybe they'll commend you for putting your life on the line in the war on drugs."

It's a war we're losing, Selena wanted to say. *Mexican meth is pouring over the border, along with heroin that is more powerful, more plentiful, and less expensive by the day. You wouldn't believe how much is coming in from Afghanistan. Don't get me going on prescription pills. And it's a war we fight with treachery and deceit, just like the bad guys. We have to think like they do. Sometimes we forget who we really are.*

"Was there something else, daughter?"

"No. No, that's all. Thank you for your kind words."

"Tell you what. You don't need a penance. But I want you to recite the Act of Hope at the start of every day for a week. Do you know it?"

"Sorry. It's been a while."

"You'll find it on a prayer card in the rack as you go out. But here it is: *O my God, relying on your almighty power and infinite mercy and promises, I hope to obtain pardon of my sins, the help of your grace, and life everlasting through the merits of Jesus Christ, my Lord and redeemer.* Think you can do that?"

"I'll give it a shot," Selena said, and then, realizing the terrible irony of her reply, burst into tears.

CHAPTER 22

She waited outside the church for the pallbearers to carry Eddie's casket the short distance to the grave site. There was no need to attend the Mass, Selena figured. Besides, a solitary and unescorted woman at a Latin funeral called too much attention to herself. She lifted her collar against the wind. Maybe it wasn't a good idea to come.

A pebbly sleet picked up, tapping her hat. It was the netted black abaca she'd bought to match the black pashmina shawl her father had brought home for her from the OPEC conference in Caracas when he was an executive with the Mexican national oil company, PEMEX. No one would be able to see her eyes behind the veil, just as at Antonio's funeral.

Red, white, and green candles flickered on stands placed around Antonio's body, covered with gladiolas, zinnias and dahlias, the Mexican national flower. An image of his namesake saint was tucked under one arm, as though he clutched it in an earnest final plea. Some of his ratchets lay in the coffin with him, but he'd bequeathed his best tools, along with the Charger, to Selena. Who knew that the Army required everyone to draw up a will, even if all you did was work the motor pool? He was in his Army dress greens, looking uncomfortable. He should have been wearing the spotted coveralls and ratty sneakers, not brand new shoes with thick rubber soles for the long road to heaven, as per Mexican custom.

The entire *familia* gathered: *tíos, tías,* including *Comadre* María, cousins, *Mamá Grande* all the way from Oaxaca. Dozens of others attended by invitation, signing in, dropping envelopes containing both *pesos* and dollars in the basket. In true *Zapotec* fashion, a hired band played slow tunes on guitars in the next room as the women wailed. Selena didn't say a word.

After the Rosary, the men began to drink tequila and Dos Equis *cerveza* in the foyer while telling stories about the deceased. A neighbor brought a prickly pear to place in the coffin for Antonio to throw at the wild bull that tries to prevent souls from crossing the plain to reach Purgatory. *Mamí* nestled it near his right hand. After the requiem Mass, the hearse, decorated with ornate bouquets and draped with lace curtains, led a procession to the *Campo Santo*, the Holy Field. In deference to Mexican custom, profuse decorations were permitted beside the grave: metal flowers and wax wreaths of all colors, made to withstand the weather.

Once the soldier presented the folded American flag from Antonio's coffin to *Mamí*, who was bent over in disbelief, Selena wept. Her *Madrina* took her hand gently and asked if she would like to touch the casket one last time with her. She did.

Afterward, she stepped away and clenched her fists in her pockets. The bugler sounded Taps. Seven riflemen fired three jolting, bolt-action volleys.

Kapow.

Kapow.

Kapow.

Back home, at 3 a.m., seventy miles an hour through West Chicago, lights off, she punched the gas on every turn and made her brother's Charger growl, her mind cleared by the rushing wind, the flash of streetlights racing past *whoop whoop whoop*, her vision blurred by speed and hot tears. When she left the suburbs and reached the open countryside, she pulled the headlamp knob and pressed her foot to the floorboard, burning rubber, surging to eighty-five, ninety, one hundred ten twenty thirty on the straightaway where Antonio dragged the *Americanos'* Camaros and Mustangs and left them all choking on his exhaust.

I'll get them, Antonio, she called out the open window over the scream of the wind, over the angry roar of The Beast's big engine. *I'll chase them all down, te lo prometo, I promise, all of them, all of them who got you hooked on that poison, my brother! I'll find a way!*

The wind howled again as she lifted her chin and peered through the black netting when the church doors groaned open and a priest, clad in black, led the party outside. Six somber *hombres* in dark suits carried Eddie to his resting place, grunting down the three concrete steps and shuffling uneasily over the frosty glaze toward the cemetery gate. Sleet danced on the coffin, trampling the dahlias fastened to the lid. By five o'clock, the streets would be iced, and people driving home from work would slide into each other's fenders. Calls, claims, adjustments, estimates, loaners. It was going to be a long night. Her secretary, Felicia, was already trying to phone her, no doubt, but Selena kept her cell off. There would be at least a dozen desperate messages waiting.

Selena fell in discreetly with the mourners, her hat brim down, veil lowered, gloved hands properly folded. Two women in front of her dabbed at their eyes with hankies. Umbrellas mushroomed, although the coughing wind forced them to be dipped halfway and held as shields. Icy needles stung Selena's face. She turned her face aside.

That's when she saw him at the church door.

Miguel.

The young man from Bragg's drug house. Bragg's little informant.

He pulled his hood over his dark hair, shoved his hands into his jeans pockets and bent into the wind. In a few steps, he disappeared around the church corner.

Selena dropped away from the parade of mourners and sank back to the cornice. She peered around it. Miguel hurried past a dumpster toward the front of the church building, slipping once on an icy patch. Selena advanced to the trash bin and ducked behind it. Miguel kept walking steadily, not glancing back. Selena slid out her hat pin, yanked off the netted hat, and tucked it under the warped dumpster lid. Good riddance. She took a folded beret from her coat pocket and pulled it on, blinking away the pelting sleet.

What was he doing here? Paying his last *respetos*? Why should he care? She rounded the dumpster and hustled to the sidewalk. At least she'd had the sense to wear the calf-high black leather shearling boots with the non-slip soles. She backed up to an ice-crusted hedge to see Miguel blend into holiday shoppers who strolled along the town's main street. The wreaths in the streetlamps shuddered. A pickup hissed by and splashed her coat. She shook off the slush and lifted her eyes to keep Miguel in sight at a comfortable interval. He weaved through other pedestrians and entered the Valu-Mart pharmacy.

She crossed the street and found refuge in the recessed doorway of the Do-It-Right hardware store. The cars that were angle-parked against the curb helped to conceal her. She pretended to eye the window merchandise, keeping watch on the pharmacy entrance. It wasn't likely he'd pass through the store; he'd gone in for cigarettes or something. If he tried to change clothes to shake a tail, she'd still spot him: they never remembered to change their shoes, and she could ID those red Converse sneakers a mile away.

A rumpled clerk in an apron came out from the hardware store, muttering about the mess on the floor, holding a yellow sack of salt. He broadcast three handfuls on the walkway, coughed into his armpit, and after stamping his feet, went back inside. Miguel stepped out, shaking a cigarette from a new pack. He cupped his hand against his Zippo, puffed, and kept walking, his cell phone clamped to his ear.

It wouldn't be hard to follow him now. He left a trail of smoke. His phone left a digital trail, too, and she made a mental note to get his calling records. What if he was calling for a ride and he climbed into a car? She'd lose him.

Was there any real point to following him? Did she really think he might lead her to The Snake, awaiting a report on the funeral? Maybe she should catch up to him and ask a few questions, like why he was at the funeral and who he was calling on the phone. Maybe she should have agreed to a backup partner in a cruiser.

A panel truck passed by, and she lost sight of him.

She squinted through the sleet, now turning to sneet, little crystals landing on her lashes. Where did he go? There — a wisp of smoke — there he was.

He remained stooped, as though preparing for a blow. But he was merely like most young men, underdressed for the cold, windy weather. No hat. No gloves.

No brains, no headaches.

Maybe he was heading for Lupita's, a Mexican café at the end of the street, where the coffee was hot and strong. She'd join him. *Fancy meeting you here, Miguel.* It wouldn't look out-of-place. They could talk there. For now, Selena stayed behind him, across the street, matching his loping pace. She checked store windows on the fly, looking like any other shopper. The beauty-salon display was full of framed portraits and mirrors. A shadow flashed across one of them, and she felt the hairs on her neck prickle.

She reached in her clutch purse for her compact. She flipped it open. Pulled aside to a wall. Lifted it to her face. A little higher. Pretended to adjust her lashes. Saw the burly man in a wool coat and ski cap leaning against a video-store window, holding a magazine up to his face much too closely.

Now there's a lame trick, she thought. And in the sleet, no less. Could be Bragg, hoping she'd lead him to the prize and he'd take the credit. She snapped the compact closed and replaced it in the purse beside her Sig Sauer. She kept the purse unlatched. Whoever was following her was more important — more of a threat — than Miguel. No use in following the little fish now. *Let's see who that big fish is, and give him a little ride.*

She entered the salon.

The gum-chewing receptionist with the spiky blue hair looked up from a magazine. "WelcometoJonesdoyouhaveanappointment?" she drawled.

"Listen," Selena said, putting on her sister-in-distress look, "there's a man outside being rude to me. I just need to know if there's a back exit."

"Oh, I get it," she said. "Lose a loser, huh?"

"It's a guy in a black wool coat and a black ski cap. If he comes in looking for me, tell him I'm in the ladies' room."

"Sure," the girl said. She cracked the gum. "Follow me. This way."

She sprang up and marched past the blowers and sinks, metallic silver Filas flashing. She paused to whisper to a blow-dried stylist snipping away at a customer. The older woman nodded and smiled sympathetically.

"Come back sometime for some gold highlights in that gorgeous hair of yours, honey," she said. "It's all the rage."

"I might," Selena said. "Thanks."

"Summer, give her a coupon, will you?" the woman said.

The young worker produced one from her vest pocket, handed it over, and pointed to the door marked with the Exit sign. "Good luck," she said.

Selena set down her handbag, shrugged off her coat while holding the ends of the sleeves, and jerked the reversible garment inside-out. It was now ash-gray. She tied up her hair in a ponytail and used an elastic band to secure it. She produced oversize Ray-Ban sunglasses and slid them on. She pulled her scarf up over her head and tied it under her chin.

"Geez," the girl said. "Looks like you've done this before."

"Once or twice," Selena said. She snatched her purse and stepped out into the alley to circle to a spot behind her tracker, her boots scrunching through crusted snow. At the sidewalk, beyond an enclosed wooden stairwell leading to the second floor, she pressed against the wet brick wall and peeked around.

He was gone.

He's gone inside, she thought. *He's asking about me now. But he won't wait inside. Men hate the smell of those places. He'll come back out.*

A slammed door. Running steps. Crunching ice.

Ay mi Dios, he's behind me.

She backed up over her footprints — two, three steps — and leaped into the covered stairwell. Drew the Sig Sauer from the handbag.

A wide man in a wool coat and ski cap walked past her, tracking her footprints to the corner of the building. He poked his head around the corner, looked left, right, and then pushed up the cap from his brow. He sighed out a foggy plume of frustration.

"Put your hands where I can see them," Selena said, "or I'll blow your head off. *¿Tengo que decirlo en español?*"

The man slowly raised his gloved hands. He understood the English command.

"Turn around so I can see you. Nice and slow."

The man turned.

Detective Gordon was bright red, and not from the cold. "For cryin' out loud, Selena, I'm real sorry about this," he said.

She lowered the pistol and removed her finger from the trigger. Caught her breath. "What's this about?"

"It's — it's just backup."

"Backup, yeah, right. Who else is with you?"

"No one."

"Really?"

"I swear."

"Tell me why you're here."

"You don't want to know."

"Don't give me that. Tell me or maybe I'll shoot anyway."

"Bragg said you might say that."

"He sent you to follow me? What for?"

"Look, I don't buy any of this —"

"Buy any of what?"

He scuffed his feet.

"What's going on here?" she pressed.

"You're not going to believe it."

"Try me."

"Bragg thinks you're the offender."

"What?"

"He says it's why you wanted to go to the funeral, and it's why you're the only woman on the list."

"You can't be serious."

He shrugged sheepishly. "He says it also explains why you're the last name on the list."

If she wasn't so angry, she might have laughed.

CHAPTER 23

The Fox snake is sick. It's not eating, and the scales near the tail's rattles look black and rotten. It hasn't moved in days. It isn't hibernating like the others. It's the cold weather. This one's a prairie native, and it shouldn't bother him. But the low temps are stressing them all.

The hot water pipes are clanking, and the heat lamps are on high, but heat rises, right? And I have to keep the humidity high. That's why the ceiling panels are fogged and dripping even as the sleet drums away at them, making a racket. And the walls — the lower panels — are twin-layer polyethylene and I hung a tarp along the outside west wall to break the wind, but it's just collecting icicles. The entire greenhouse is insulated pretty well, don't get me wrong: I had to caulk every possible hole and weatherstrip every crevice to make the room escape-proof. Hot snakes are all Houdinis. That's why I have the best cages you can get. But these glass vivariums don't warm up well, and the metal frames are cool to my touch. I mean, I can't cover every single drafty hole in the place. The cement floor has drains and there's a double-screened vent over the door I covered with those plastic sheets you seal with a hair dryer.

I put the portable propane heater near my favorites, the Mexican desert vipers and the barba amarilla, of course. He's the only one I'm afraid of. No wonder Mexicans know him as El Diablo. The Devil.

The flowers don't need the extra heat; they're tougher than the cold-blooded reptiles. The mums are hardy, and the marigolds don't mind the chill. The amaryllis looks good. My shrub roses

Viper

prefer it cool, and I bred the white winter roses for this. The dahlias are fine. But the snakes — well, I'd move them out to the middle of the room, but then they might be seen by a casual visitor. Not that I ever get any visitors since the new greenhouses were built. But if someone wandered in, they'd freak out.

Why are so many people afraid of snakes? Most are harmless. And these — these are elegant and efficient, hermoso y peligroso, yes, beautiful and dangerous, that is it. And ancient. Descended from that great sea serpent Leviathan, the lord of chaos. The Bible says so.

It must go back to that Eden thing, too. But wasn't the serpent the most clever of creatures? Did he not succeed in seducing the first human woman, Eve, with smooth talk? Was she not like the beautiful virgin Xochiquetzal, who ate the forbidden fruit from the aphrodisiac tree and submitted to temptation? This is why she was thrown down from Paradise and can no longer look directly into the sky. This is why her soft eyes are always lowered and her head is covered by a blue veil speckled with marigolds, because they look like the stars she left behind in the heavens.

O Xochiquetzal, virgin and mother of us all, hear me: It is well you are honored on the Day of the Dead as the goddess who brought both death and life into the world. It is proper that your flower, the marigold, is spread on the graves of our ancestors at the first new moon after harvest. For then we are reminded how fragile we are, like flowers — and also reminded of the golden stars, where we will live forever if we are devoted to you and offer you sacrifices, as you know I have done.

Can you hear that? It's the sleet clattering louder. They say it will stop soon. No matter. I know when the next new moon will arise to mark the end of this present age, and the New Age will begin, ruled by Coatlicue, Queen Mother of the Divine Sun. Great Mother of gods, why do your people not celebrate you? They have forgotten you, with your glorious skirt of rattlesnakes and your fearsome necklace of human hearts and skulls of your enemies. They have forgotten everything. Everything! Great Coatlicue, you are the one to be honored and prayed to, not that other one, that — that impostor imported by the conquistadores to fool the Aztecas. Our Lady of Guadalupe. Ha! She is only human and cannot overcome you, Coatlicue, mother of gods.

Especially on your sacred night, when you receive the virgin I will offer to you.

You know the one.

CHAPTER 24

Selena slammed back the slide of the P226 Sig Sauer, let it snap back into place, extended her arms, and, double-handed, squeezed all fifteen rounds into the paper target. She released the empty magazine and rammed in another, ears ringing. The firing-range earmuffs were snug, but she'd forgotten how loud the report could be. Her wrists felt rubbery. It had been a long time.

"Can you tell I've been away from it for a while?" she asked, a bit too loudly.

"Two months without practice, and I suck," Gordon called back.

"What am I doing wrong?"

"Hard to tell," Gordon said, adjusting his protective glasses. "The shots missing to the left tell me you're turning the barrel that way when you pull the trigger. Doesn't take much to be off. And the shots missing high tell me you're anticipating the recoil and pulling your arms back to soften the kick. Focus on the sight, not the target."

"Even if I pretend it's Bragg?" she said, squatting, presenting, and firing. Powpowpowpowpow. A hot shell bounced off the brim of her White Sox cap.

"Whaddya think?" she called.

"Not bad. For a girl."

She shot him a look, straightened her finger, lowered the pistol, and took a breather. She coughed away the gritty gunpowder smoke. "It's like riding a bike, right? Tell me you get it back."

"You get it back."

She took her stance, left foot forward, right anchored. *Steady. Steady. Stop shaking. Squeeze.*

Pow.

Pow.

Pow.

Pow.

CLICK.

"What happened?" she asked. Then she saw the shell stuck in the slide.

"That's what I hate about semiautomatics," Gordon said with a sniff. "They jam easy. Double-feeds, stovepiping. Just like you have there. Give it a good whack and rack it."

Selena thumped the grip from below and swept back the slide to release the empty shell stuck there and to chamber the next one.

"How many rounds left?" Gordon asked.

Selena shrugged. "I'm not sure."

"You gotta be sure," Gordon said. "You gotta count out loud to yourself. The bad guy will be counting your shots. You *have* forgotten a lot, huh?"

"I guess so," she agreed. The Academy training was a long time ago: stance, draw, grip, strong-hand shots, weak-hand shots, reload while running. She was glad she'd de-greased the five-pound trigger assembly and lubed it. At least she remembered how to do *that*. "My best shot was a time in New Mexico when I blew away a sidewinder rattler at full speed after it crawled out one of my boots in the morning and then tried to get away. I've hated snakes since."

"So how many shots left?" Gordon insisted.

"I don't know, OK? I don't know."

"You have six left. Those are all the shots I get in my .38 Special. No need to get snippy. Next time you won't have anyone to tell you."

"Sorry."

"It's fine. What are friends for, huh?"

Selena secured her firearm, pulled off the muffs and removed her safety glasses. "Now: explain how Bragg convinced you that I'm the bad guy."

Gordon exhaled laboriously as though he was carrying a full field desert pack with hydration bags. He glanced around, furtive as a finch in a neighborhood known for its cats. The outdoor firing range seemed to be the most private place to talk. No one would think to look for them here. And if they did, they'd say Selena asked for a little practice, just as Bragg had suggested.

"I'd better start from the beginning," Gordon said with a nervous cough. "We had a series of animal killings in spring and early summer. It started small and went up. Chickens. Then stray cats and dogs left outside at night. Eviscerated sheep. At first we figured we were dealing with coyotes. They've made a comeback in Illinois and have been a problem for farmers, even for joggers in the Forest Preserves. But there wasn't much eaten. Coyotes wouldn't do that."

"Someone was practicing."

"Working his way up," Gordon concurred, "and building his nerve. We checked with area vets and the humane-society people to find any patterns."

"Find any?"

"The size of the animals increased, and they were all de-gutted. The killings were all within a seventy-five-mile radius of River Falls, more or less. So it's gotta be a local."

"Then the human killing began."

"Around the middle of August. It was hard to make any connection at first. You know how gangs have moved in all these small towns to deal drugs with immigrant workers at the canneries and farm operations, huh? So ya get your rivalries, turf fights, drive-bys and knifings in deals gone bad. All in a day's work."

"Another reason I got out of it," Selena said. The so-called war on drugs never ended. "So what tipped you off?"

"The flowers left on the bodies."

"Someone was signing his work."

"Or *her* work. We heard from Father Johnny that this 'Blue Lady' was making announcements about men being killed and how his parishioners thought it was the Virgin Mary leaving flowers on the bodies of dopers as her signature. When he came in soon after Halloween and showed us the Book of the Deceased and we saw how it listed six dealers killed this way, we called the State Police — cross-county jurisdiction and all that — the FBI, and the DEA."

"So where's the FBI? Don't they have a Special Agent assigned to the case?"

"They did, but Bragg told him to back off. Said he knew all these guys, and, of course, there was the last name on the list."

"Mine."

"Bragg said you were a former agent and not a dealer like the others, which was odd. As soon as we figured out you'd changed your name, I told Bragg about how you had a part in the case last spring with Father Ray's murder and that fellow Stubblefield. Say, are you two seeing each other or what?"

Selena drilled her eyes into him. "What's it to you?"

"OK, sorry. None of my beeswax."

Selena drew a breath and tugged her hat brim down. Had she been too harsh with Reed? It was for his own safety. Would she see him again? Get lost in those dreamy sea-gray eyes? Hear his jokes that made her giggle like a schoolgirl? "So that's how Bragg found me," Selena said, her voice even and cool.

"Bragg suspected you from the beginning and told us to shut up and to keep an eye on you. Sure, The Snake knew all those victims. But so did you."

"So what?"

"The last name — yours — could be a *signature*, he said, not part of the victim list."

Selena rolled her eyes. "I still can't believe this. So, what's my motive?"

"Setting things right. Frustration over a career that, well, didn't end up the way you wanted. You decided to take matters into your own hands because all these guys didn't get the punishment they deserved. He told us you've had a big hang-up over it since your brother —"

"Leave my brother out of this."

Gordon sniffed. He looked down at his shoes. "Look, it's getting cold out here. Do you think maybe we could go in —"

"Did he really think I could kill these guys so brutally, and blame it on The Snake?" Selena spat, her blood boiling.

"You might have an accomplice, he says. You know a lot of people in the Latin community here with your insurance agency and literacy work. Slaughterhouse workers could do it easily for a price or a favor. They're used to the blood."

"How could he possibly believe I'd be involved in such a thing?"

"He said you call yourself — let me remember — 'La Broo-ha,' did I pronounce it right? A witch?"

She laughed derisively. "As a joke, because Bragg says I'm a pushy broad. Did he really convince you that I'd be a witch promising gang members magical protection from bullets by offering human sacrifices? They already have Jesus Malverde, the unofficial patron saint of drug traffickers, for that."

"No kidding?"

"He's kind of a Robin Hood bandit from the early 1900s. He's for mid-level dopers. The poorer ones pray to Saint Death and the Virgin of Guadalupe."

"Yeah, well, speaking of her, Bragg suggested you could be The Blue Lady, too."

"This is almost funny," she said, fuming.

" 'Look at the instant connection with Jacinta,' Bragg said to us. Like you'd met before. Jacinta acted like she recognized you. But you have a solid alibi for the last apparition, at your office all day and working on that car of yours nearly all night."

"How would you know?"

Gordon shrugged, and sputtered, "Aw, you know."

"You guys staked me out?"

"For me, that surveillance took you off the hook." His teeth chattered. "And b-by the way, that car looks great. Charger, is it? What year?"

"Sixty-nine. So you think I'm OK, huh?"

"Yeah, but Bragg still isn't sure. B-but the question still bugs me: Why are you the only woman on the list, and the last n-name?"

"I'm the only woman The Snake has a grudge against, and I was the last one to betray him before he was jailed. That's why. It's that simple."

"Then why isn't Bragg on the list?"

"The killer is targeting only Hispanics. It's blood revenge. What I don't understand yet is why The Snake is doing it in a ritualistic way. Working through a list. Leaving flowers. And this whole Blue Lady business."

"So this Blue Lady is acting as his surrogate. Could even be The Snake in a disguise, the girl being ordered by The Snake to kill them."

"She's just an abused little girl," Selena shot back. "She couldn't possibly overcome these men."

"Alright, alright," Gordon conceded, "you don't need to bite my head off."

"Y'know, with missing organs, especially a heart, we have a sign for a religious motive," Selena suggested. "Like a sacrifice."

"Think The Snake got religion like that in prison?"

"Doubtful. The only religion he ever had was himself and his turf. And so what if the hit list was part of a church's Book of the Deceased? That was a cheap publicity stunt." Still, she wondered. Was it to enhance his reputation among lesser dealers or announce to the Big Boys in Chicago that he was in their league after all?

Gordon drew in a sharp breath and sneezed. "Oh, great. A cold coming on. Look, can we go? I'm f-freezing."

"Sure. You go ahead. I'll be right there." She slipped the pistol into her snap purse and trotted out to the range, where she unclipped the paper targets from the line.

She found her thoughts echoing the smoky-voiced profiling instructor at the Academy, a grizzled wavy-haired psychology professor who stabbed his unlit pipe at students while he lectured:

The typical profile of a religiously motivated multiple murderer is a male or female who is disturbed, yes, but creative, highly imaginative, even artistic. They are intelligent yet often under-achievers who suffer low self-esteem and have suffered peer or family rejection. They feel they are persecuted. They blend into normal society quietly and do not appear to be odd. They have apartments and jobs; they go to school and they go to church. They drive late-model cars. They are organized, paying attention to detail when planning out their fantasies — as opposed to a disorganized, impulsive, and sloppy killer. They can be as young as 13, rarely over 24. They are often the oldest sibling. Many are visionaries who hear voices and obey instructions.

Many are visionaries who hear voices and obey instructions. Many are visionaries who hear voices and obey instructions.

It can't be Jacinta. *As young as 13.* No. Not her.

When she joined Gordon at the unmarked police Impala, she leaned on the roof on the driver side. Gordon had the heat and fan running on high.

Gordon blew his nose. He had a real trumpet. "So what are we gonna do now?" he asked, tucking away the handkerchief.

"With Bragg out of the way for a while, I'll do some poking around on my own. Did he go back to Chicago, or is he still around?"

"He said he was going home to the city."

"Just as well," Selena said. "If Bragg calls you about me, tell him I'm busy as heck at my insurance office, dealing with all the accidents from today's awful weather. It won't be far from the truth."

"Sure. But what's the plan after that?"

"First, I want to visit Miguel," Selena said. "I want to know why he was at the funeral, for one thing, and who he was talking to on the phone. Maybe he'll have some leads for me."

"That's what I've been hoping," Gordon said. "No one's been talking to us cops. They're afraid we're gonna arrest them on immigration charges even though we have no authority to do it. Not in Illinois, anyway."

"That's another good reason for me to visit Jacinta by myself, if I can find her alone." The last meeting, with the sudden disappearance, disturbed her. Still — "I think she trusts me. Maybe she'll introduce me to The Blue Lady. I think once we find out who The Blue Lady really is, we'll find The Snake or have the real offender."

Gordon released the emergency brake. "What if it's actually the Virgin Mary?"

"You believe that?"

"Nah. I'm not religious. You?"

"What? Believe it?"

"Yeah," Gordon said. "You religious?"

"Everyone has faith in something," she said, placing the Sig Sauer in her purse.

Gordon's car radio squawked, and he picked up the handset. "Gordon here, go ahead. Uh-huh. Huh? Well, if that isn't a turn. I'm on it."

He replaced the handset. "Before he left, Bragg took a look at the phone number used to call Eddie. It may be registered to a Carlos Ventura, but it's the number Bragg always used to call Miguel. Miguel's at the house now, packing up his stuff. He says he's through with us."

"Not yet," Selena said. "Now we've got two reasons to talk to him," Selena said. "I'll meet you there. We'd better step on it."

She leaped into the Jeep and wished she had the Charger. *Could make it in half the time*, she thought. *Even then, it might be too late.*

CHAPTER 25

Once Selena screeched up to Miguel's place, she double-checked the Sig Sauer and tucked the purse securely under her arm. *Six rounds.*

She stepped out of the car, joined Gordon at the sidewalk, and headed for the front steps. "He's not exactly conscientious about shoveling, is he?" she said. The corrugated soles of her black leather shearling boots left detailed impressions in the rime, and she noticed her prints weren't the only ones coming and going.

She clicked her heels to loosen snow and rapped on the door. It creaked open.

"Funny," she said. "I remember he unlocked it from the inside when those other *hombres* visited."

"Young guy. Forgets stuff like that," Gordon said.

"Miguel?" Selena called through the crack. "Miguel, are you here?"

Nothing.

She kicked it open. *"¿Miguel? ¿Estás aquí?"*

She stepped inside.

A shriek pierced her ears. She dropped to a duck, groping for a holster that wasn't there.

The cat bounded across the room, leaping over a table and spilling a can of Mountain Dew.

She held her hand against her heart. *Can't keep the Sig Sauer in the purse anymore,* she thought.

"I don't like this," Gordon said. He drew his service revolver.

"You hear anything?" she asked. A voice, a radio, a television, footsteps, anything. Just the tabby mewing on the way to the kitchen. She crossed to it.

There he was — propped in a chrome-and-vinyl chair, bound with laundry line, mouth duct-taped, throat gashed and belly bared with two crosses carved across it. *Double-cross.*

She dashed to his side and checked for a pulse on his wrist with two joined fingers. But the bluish pallor told her he'd been gone for a while, perhaps since he returned from the funeral.

Gordon held his revolver in a high ready position, a two-handed grip against his chest, his narrowed eyes darting back and forth. "Get out of here, Selena," Gordon ordered, his voice low. "There still might be someone in the house."

"No way," she said, hauling her pistol out. "Let's do a search."

"I'm calling in some backup first," Gordon said, fumbling for his phone, still glancing around as though expecting an ambush. "Don't touch anything. Hey — where you going?"

Selena held a finger to his lips and jerked her head *let's go.* Gordon pocketed his phone.

"Fine," he whispered. "But I go first and clear left, you follow and clear right. Got it?"

"And if you feel a sneeze coming on, you back out."

"Deal."

They searched the rooms in silence, ducking in and out of doorways, weapons at the ready, fingers off the triggers. They flung open closets and ducked under beds. They checked the shower. Peeked into the surveillance room with the camera set-up and two-way mirror. Descended to the basement where Selena wished she had a flashlight attachment for the Sig. Satisfied that the house was clear, Gordon blew his nose and made his call.

"Paramedics and techies will be here in a few minutes," he said with a sniffle. "Not much we can do until everyone shows up."

"There is one thing," Selena said. "Let's check the cameras."

They returned to the surveillance room. "The funeral was at 11 a.m.," Selena noted. "It got out at noon. He did his little walk-around and drove back here, or caught a ride back here, while we were at the range."

"So we just need to see footage from about 1:30 on. Let's see if he walks in with someone or if he was ambushed by someone waiting here. Lemme find it. I've run this equipment before."

Gordon took a seat and typed on a keyboard. A black and white image shuddered on the monitor. "OK, here's the living room and entryway and the time signature says 1:30," he said, squinting at the picture. "You'd think with the money you Drug Enforcement people confiscate you could afford a better camera and set-up."

"Can you speed it up until we see someone walking in?"

"Sure." With two clicks, the image blinked in rapid fast forward. A shadow appeared and Gordon tapped the keyboard. The image slowed to normal and the figure emerged from silhouette, making a rude gesture at the camera. It was Miguel.

"There's our boy," Gordon said. "He looks like he's alone and in a hurry."

"I can tell you why," Selena said. "The word is out on the street that he's a rat — something he learned or confirmed at the funeral, probably — and he needs to get out of this house *pronto*. Don't we have sound on this?"

"Oh, yeah. Let's see — here." Gordon clicked an icon. But as soon as Miguel scurried past the camera range, the sound died.

"Directional mic," Gordon said. "We won't hear anything in the kitchen."

But they did. An argument. A struggle. The crash of a chair. A man's voice cursing. English? Spanish? Hard to tell. Selena leaned closer to the speakers. One man? More? Who else had access to the house? Police officers like Baker and Bragg, who would be angry with Miguel for jeopardizing his sting. No, it couldn't be Bragg. No way. Dumb idea: Bragg popping these guys one at a time? Or making arrangements to have it done? By Miguel? Then silencing Miguel? No. Well — Besides, Bragg knew about the camera set-up here and wouldn't risk exposure.

The sounds stopped. Miguel was dead by now or close to it. Shadows played at the corner of the screen. The full figure of a burly male stepped into the frame and headed briskly for the front door, tugging up his collar. He was Bragg's height and build, all right, complete with crew cut. Bragg would make it look like gang vengeance, Selena thought, taking all suspicion off himself. But unless he turned around there wouldn't be a way to ID him for sure.

Then he spun and called to the kitchen. "*¡Vamos!*" The face was sepia, the mustache thick as a push broom. Another man entered the frame, back to the camera, and the two slipped outside.

"Run that back," Selena said.

"I'm on it," Gordon answered, tapping the keyboard. The herky-jerky figures re-entered the room backward, and at the point where the first man turned, Gordon hit pause. He zoomed in.

"Know this guy?" he asked. "Lemme zoom in a little more. Might lose resolution, though. There. How's that?"

Selena leaned close to the flickering screen. Where had she seen him before?

"Can you tilt down to his shoes?" she asked.

"Always with the shoes, huh?"

She gave him a look.

He dragged and clicked the mouse. "How's that? Black cowboy boots, it looks like."

"Full quill black ostrich with wingtips," she said.

"Sounds pricey."

"That's one of the guys who came to the station with Miss Sandoval. Those are his boots. The other guy is probably the man who accompanied him."

A bang at the front door startled them. The paramedics burst in.

"Showtime," Gordon said, rising from the swivel chair. "I'll look after things here, Selena."

"Say, can you print that frame?"

"Yeah, no problem. Later I'll go back farther and see if we can get a better shot of them arriving." He pressed some keys, and a printer whirred.

"I'll visit Eva Sandoval with this," Selena said. " Maybe she'll tell us who these guys are and where to find them. I think they're her brothers who live with her."

"Good luck with that."

"I'd better go home and freshen up a bit. I'll take the Charger to visit Sandoval. It can have the effect of a cocked shotgun in a raid."

The black-and-white print spit out, and Gordon handed it to her. He punched her in the shoulder. "You be careful, huh?"

CHAPTER 26

When Selena rounded the corner of her street, she noticed the Christmas decor strung on neighbors' shrubs and eaves. It was too early in the day to see lights, but doors sported wreaths and Santa Claus cutouts, while lawns displayed sleighs, reindeer, and plastic snowmen. She hadn't even started decorating and wouldn't until the novena before *Noche-buena*, Christmas Eve. During the nine days of the *posadas*, she and her brothers had paraded through the neighborhood each night with all the other kids, in bright costumes, holding candles and singing Mexican carols with guitars and, in imitation of Joseph and Mary, asking neighbors if they can stay. The first two always refused, and the third took them inside, where there was already a barn scene set up. Everyone prayed the Rosary in Spanish, the *Santa Marías* rolling like soft waves. Afterward, they partied with *piñatas*, fritters, and fresh fruit drinks like *horchata*, *chía*, and *piña*. One time Lorenzo got into the men's *tequila* supply somehow and spent the rest of the night kneeling in front of the toilet.

This year I'm going to keep it simple, she thought, parking at the curb. *Candles in the windows as usual, garland on the banisters. I'll set up the pesebre with the carved olive-tree figures of the whole nativity scene.*

Her family had a large set in the living room and each person had a little crèche in their rooms. Every year someone disappeared from the big set-up; if it wasn't Saint Joseph, it was a shepherd or a magi. One year they couldn't find the Baby Jesus. Selena cried because she thought there wouldn't be a Christmas that year because of it. The Baby Jesus turned up in time, albeit with tiny bite marks from *Mami's* Chihuahua. Selena was still missing a magi from her own set, the one carrying the gold. *Maybe this year I'll find him*, she mused with a soft chuckle. *But then who else will disappear?*

The *familia* always gathered at Comadre María's. First, Christmas midnight Mass, then chow down at *Madrina's*. Her mouth watered thinking of the colorful *bacalao a la vizcaina* and *romeritos* in *mole* sauce. *This mess had better be over with by then,* she muttered as she stepped out and trotted to the front door.

Still plenty of light left in the day. She checked her watch, thinking she didn't have time to think about presents. Anyway, family gifts weren't given until Epiphany, *Dia de los Santos Reyes Magos.* Reed might expect something at Christmas, though. There was the cognac she bought for a special occasion. Maybe that. But would she see him again at all? Her heart squeezed like a *limón.*

She jingled her keys, found the one for the front door, and plunged it in, rushing through a mental list: *bundle up, it's getting cold. After changing, drive to the office, get the Charger and race down I-88 to Prophetstown. Do I need to get gas? Take the GPS just in case I get lost even if I was there before. Check with Felicia about office calls.*

She shouldered against the door but it didn't budge. The deadbolt was engaged. *Don't remember doing that,* she thought. Glancing over her shoulder furtively, she leaned her body on the door frame and fingered the keychain again, opened the door, and stepped inside.

A glass tinkled in the kitchen.

Someone was in the house.

Madre de Dios, they went for Miguel first, and now they're here.

She backed to the wall and drew her pistol from the purse. She set the purse down and double-fisted the Sig Sauer against her thumping chest. She padded toward the kitchen, her mouth suddenly dry. A cup scraped on a countertop.

She lunged into the kitchen, gun high.

The man dropped the metal cup. It clinked on the tile and splashed.

Lorenzo gawked at her, mouth agape. "Holy *tamales,* Selena, you still have that thing? You almost gave me a heart attack. What were you thinking? And don't you have any beer in the house?"

Selena let out a puffy breath and lowered the pistol. "Lorenzo, what are you doing here?"

"Now that you're here, you can make me some lunch. I'm starving."

"I'm not doing any such thing."

"You don't even have stuff for my favorite, scrambled eggs and hot dogs. You've got the ketchup and Tabasco sauce for it, but you don't have —"

Selena stuffed the gun in her belt. "Elena kicked you out again, didn't she?"

"Kicked? Well, I dunno about *kicked* —"

"What this time? Seeing someone on the side again?"

"I dunno about *seeing* —"

Selena stooped to a cabinet, seized a spray cleaner, and tore off three sheets of paper towel. She wiped up the spill and gave it a sniff. "This is Margarita mix," she said.

"Yeah, well, like I told you, you have no beer and so I —"

"It's the middle of the afternoon."

"Look, you gonna make me something or no?"

"You deserve an iguana on a stick."

"I like barbeque."

"Pig."

"I like that, too." He swayed.

"How much of this did you drink?"

"Not enough yet."

"You've had plenty." She tossed the damp paper towels, plunked the cup in the sink, and ran her hands under the faucet. "You used to run home to *Mama-cita* and now you run to me? Is that it? What do you want me to do? Tuck you in bed and bring you a glass of warm milk with a splash of coffee like *Mamí* used to do?"

"I just need a few days, you know, for Elena to come to her senses."

"Oh, *really?*" Selena huffed. "*Escúchame*, Lorenzo, and listen up good: you can't stay here. This is not a good time at all. Not at all." It's too *dangerous*, she wanted to say and couldn't.

"Have a heart, sis," Lorenzo pleaded. "I'll be good. I won't throw up on the couch like last time."

"I can't talk about this now," Selena said, waving her hands. "I have to go. I'm going to my office and then on some calls."

"So like, can you bring back some beer?"

"Drive yourself to the *mercado*."

"I can't. I didn't drive down. Francisco said he'd drive me if I loaned him a hundred bucks and paid for the gas. So he drove me down here and left."

"Then walk. There's a gas station six blocks that way."

"Yeah, right," he snorted. "Me, walk?"

"I'm going upstairs to change and then I'm leaving. When I'm gone, don't let anyone in the house. Got it?"

"Sure," Lorenzo said. "Hey, who's this Reed guy who keeps calling for you? Do you mean him? You got a *gringo* boyfriend now?"

She stopped. "You talked to him?"

"He just leaves messages. I don't pick up."

She hurried upstairs and punched the messages button on her answering machine.

"Selena, it's Reed. I'll be in town next week and hoped that maybe I could see you, just for coffee or something. Go out for Chinese? I'll try again later. Bye for now."

Four messages, the same, more or less, each time. "I miss you," he said after the fourth.

Her finger hovered over the speed-dial button, and then she curled her fingers into a fist. *I can't. Not yet.*

She jumped into black jeans, pulled on her buckled Minnetonkas, layered two sweaters, and snatched her black trench coat on the way out, past her begging brother: "And chips! We need chips!"

CHAPTER 27

Selena parked the Charger outside Sandoval's tenement and frowned when the engine grumbled and sighed after she turned off the ignition. The Beast needed tuning again. Maybe she could delay that with a quart of liquid titanium additive. Maybe she could burn off carbon and dried-up gas with a roaring quarter-mile run. More likely, though, she'd have to get under the hood later to check the carburetor's air-bleed jets, main jets, and emulsion tubes for dirt.

She levered out, slammed the door, and patted her chest to feel the photo in the vest pocket that she planned to show Eva Sandoval. The woman had been friendly enough before. Maybe she'd invite her inside this time. Maybe Jacinta was here.

Selena ascended the steps, exhaled loudly, and then knocked. Eva Sandoval threw open the door, a bouquet of blue dahlias, the Mexican national flower, cradled in her elbow.

For a second Eva squinted at Selena. "What are *you* doing here again?" she said shortly, her moon-shaped face pinched. "I told you I'd call if Jacinta wanted lessons."

"I'm not here to see Jacinta," Selena assured her, taken aback.

"What do you want, then? Do you mind? I'm busy with an assignment for school."

"You came to the *policía* station with two men. I need to know who they are."

"Why?"

"Relatives of yours? Do they live here?"

"You want to sell them insurance?"

Selena whipped out the photo. "Recognize this man?"

"What if I do?"

"This is one of the men who accompanied you to the station."

I never forget a shoe, she thought.

"And the other *hombre*," Selena continued, "with his back to the camera, is probably the other who was with you, *no?*"

"Where was this taken?"

"Security camera near the scene of a crime," Selena said. "I need to talk to them as possible witnesses."

The woman's face hardened. "So you are working with the police, after all. I have nothing to say," Eva said, pushing the door shut with her bare Indian foot, red as Puebla pottery. "Go back to your police *amigos*."

"You really want me to talk to my police *amigos?*" Selena asked, a hand pressed to the door. "They'll find out who else lives here, and their real names, and, shall I say, 'status'?" Selena pushed against the door a bit more. "You really want me to do that?"

Eva stopped pushing the door.

Selena tapped her Minnetonkas. "Their names, *por favor*, and where I can find them."

"They are with everyone else, following Jacinta," she said, flicking her wrist. "She is having another one of her stupid visions. The crowd should be easy to find. They're probably at the Riverside Cemetery. And the names — ask them yourself."

"I will," Selena said. "Oh, one other thing."

"What is it now?"

"Nice flowers for a school assignment."

The woman rolled her eyes. "Like I told you, it's homework. I'm taking a flower-arranging course at Sinnissippi Community College. Now get out."

CHAPTER 28

Jacinta knelt between two marble monuments, her ecstatic face tilted up toward a stand of burr oaks, hands clasped, biting her lip. Her dun coat fanned out behind her like a cape, and her brown wool stocking cap barely covered her ears, the lobes reddened with cold. Her measured breath steamed from her open mouth. A thick and silent crescent of onlookers stood several feet apart from her, fingering rosaries, holding up candles and framed images of Our Lady of Guadalupe. Some coats had the image embroidered on the backs.

Selena circled to the edge of the crowd, studying the treetops. Nothing there but a few brittle leaves chattering in the breeze. And the only voices were the murmuring *Aves* of the faithful. She noticed Father Johnny Sullivan taking a picture, and she approached him.

"How long does it last?" she asked quietly.

The priest pocketed the camera. "The locution? Usually ten minutes, sometimes thirty or more. This is her longest one so far."

"Aren't we supposed to see something?"

"No," he said, the voice low. "Only the seers are granted the vision."

"Huh," Selena whispered with a note of doubt.

"In approved apparitions, something else happens to convince people. The dancing sun at Fatima, or the healing of terminal illnesses, or the roses that bloomed in December when Juan Diego saw Our Lady of Guadalupe, and of course, the image impressed on his *tilma* — that we can still see clearly after five hundred years. That's a miracle in itself."

"How do we know she's not faking it? Or she's self-deluded or just disturbed?"

"We don't know for sure," Father Johnny replied. "It's why I'm here taking notes and pictures. I want to be ready when the diocesan commission gets here. You know, these things need to be carefully documented, and witnesses need to be interviewed. Any alleged miracles must be investigated carefully. Most apparitions take years before they are approved. Others are never approved, even popular ones drawing thousands of pilgrims, like those in Medjugorje, in Bosnia."

"Guess I'll cancel my trip, then."

"The visionaries there are getting older and no longer seeing anything, anyway. Visionaries are almost always very young, like Jacinta, not well educated, not known for being especially spiritual prior to the visions."

"Looks like she's about to say something now."

The crowd rustled. Mobile devices flipped open to record the event and a camcorder or two hummed. Father Johnny retrieved his digital camera and set it to "movie." Jacinta was on her feet, surveying the crowd with a serene, even beatific, visage. Her fawn eyes brightened, and she lifted both hands as though in benediction.

"*La señora dice oren, ah oren, mis niños,*" she began in a small voice. "The Lady says: Pray, oh pray, my children. How can you hope to see my Son in heaven if you do not speak to him while on earth? So repent and put aside everything that keeps you from prayer. The devil is a serpent."

Selena leaned to listen.

"*La Serpiente* means to deceive you and devour you."

Selena felt a chill in her back. Was Jacinta talking directly to her?

"*Oren*, oh pray you will not fall to his lies. Those who follow him and, like him, deceive and destroy my people will die. You know who you are. There is still time to repent."

A man bolted from the crowd and ran for the cemetery gate. Selena caught a glimpse of him.

"*Ay, mi Dios,*" Selena said. "It's him."

It was Oscar Orozco, the man who was next to last in the Book of the Deceased list.

"Who?" Father Johnny said, but Selena was already weaving through the crowd, serpentine, her eyes on Oscar as he burst out of the group of onlookers, nearly pushing over a woman. The men with her had a few choice words for him. Selena pressed past them and called after the fleeing man.

"Oscar," she shouted, *"¡Espera!* Wait!"

Oscar didn't look back. He hurried through the gate, jumped into a rusty Ford pickup, and screeched away.

Selena felt about for her phone. *Call Gordon. Get an APB out. Oh, no. Where is it?* Her stomach twisted. The phone was in the purse, in the Charger. "*No, no, no, no,*" she slapped her forehead and scolded herself, *"Selena, que mensa eres."* She dashed to the car, leaped into it and peeled off with a deafening roar and a high-pitched squeal of burning rubber.

The pickup truck passed three cars, forcing oncoming vehicles into the curb, blaring their horns. Selena punched the gas, and the Charger howled forward. She flew through the opening the man had made just as he ran a red light and made a hard left.

He knew she was on his tail.

A FedEx truck entered the intersection, blocking her way.

She jammed on the brakes. The Charger screamed to a stop. The truck passed, and Selena recollected her racetrack training. *Don't stomp to the floor. Make it smooth; you'll catch up.* She pressed the gas pedal. The car growled and leaped, the tires spewing smoke behind her. *Too much gas. Don't spin. No traction.*

She pushed the accelerator more deliberately. Where was he? Where? *No, no, no, no. Think like them. Where would I go? Another turn? No, he's not thinking at all. He's scared to death. He's just heading out of town. Stay straight.*

And there he was. Selena gripped the steering wheel at the ten-to-three position, streaked past a van, and swerved back just in time to avoid an oncoming car. The road, following the Sinnissippi River, began to get curvy, with trees blocking the view around corners. She drew behind him and blew her horn. He sped up instead of pulling over, tires whining around a curve. *Idiota,* she breathed. Selena felt the spike in force as the car's weight transferred around the bend and pendulumed back. She lifted off the throttle to increase the grip of the front wheels, and then accelerated to ride his bumper. She flashed her headlights. No result. Oscar screamed around a curve, fishtailing, and for a moment Selena feared he'd tip or spin into the river.

She'd have to force him off the road. She released her white-knuckled right hand from the steering wheel and patted around for her purse. She looked down for a split second to locate it and jerked the car back into the lane when a horn bugled. A Chevy whooshed past, the driver shouting at her.

She fished out the pistol and gunned the bellowing engine. *Dios, me ayuda, please help me, God.* She tugged the steering wheel left to draw alongside the pickup and yanked it back when a car in her lane whistled around the curve. *Ay, too close.* The road straightened. *Now or never. Wait for that oncoming car. Wait. Wait.*

It sped by.

Go.

She veered into the left lane again and roared beside the truck. She aimed the Sig Sauer at Oscar through the closed window and wiggled the gun. *Pull over,* she mouthed, thinking *And please don't make me blow out an expensive window.* Suddenly he looked terrified. She saw why.

A semi was heading straight for her.

She feathered the brakes to avoid locking them and pulled right with a horrible screech, falling behind the pickup just as the semi thundered by, blasting its horn.

Selena moved left again and rocketed alongside the pickup. She aimed the gun again at Oscar's head.

He slowed and angled the truck off the pavement.

Selena passed him, steered into the gravel shoulder and squeezed the brakes hard down-up, down-up to avoid a spin-out. She thrust the car into reverse and the wheels kicked up a cloud of gray dust. She stopped, jumped out, and ran to the pickup, gun ready. She felt lightheaded and her breath was quick, but she managed to shout, "¡Oscar, no to voy a hacer daño! I'm not going to hurt you! Oscar, I want to help you!"

Oscar Orozco pressed his forehead to his steering wheel, shuddering. Selena worried for a moment that he might panic and dash off. Was he armed?

"Get out of the truck, Oscar," she called, gun lowered but ready. "I just want to talk."

The truck door creaked open, and Oscar stepped down to the gravel. His legs were rubbery, and he dropped to his knees. "*¡Entonces es verdad,*" he cried, "I said I wouldn't believe it unless I heard it for myself! It is true! So you also have come to see for yourself?"

She ignored the question. "What do you think is true, Oscar?"

"*La Serpiente* has sent *Santa Muerte*, Saint Death, after us. He made confession and for his penance he revealed all our names in the Book of the Deceased, and *La Señora de Las Sombras*, The Lady of Shadows, she announces through this girl the time for the next one to die."

"Are you kidding?" Selena said. "The Snake devoted to the patron saint of traffickers? And Lady Death speaking through this innocent little girl? Are you *loco?*"

"She said there is time to repent. If I can find a shrine to *Santa Muerte* and leave her cigarettes and flowers, she will not harm me."

"Calm down and come to your senses, Oscar," Selena said. "Since you know who all the other victims have been, you know full well that it's all of us who offended *La Serpiente* somehow. He's out of prison and picking us off one at a time. It's just payback."

Oscar blinked at her and laughed. "Is that what you think? You should know better than that."

"What do you mean?"

"You know how badly he wanted to be an associate of The Barracuda through you."

"Yeah. So what?"

"So now he is. He didn't need to go through you after all."

"What are you talking about?"

"Aren't you still working with The Barracuda? I can't believe you don't know."

"Don't know what? Out with it or I'll change my mind about the gun."

"He's working with The Barracuda," Oscar said. "In Mexico. Haven't you been told?"

Her heart constricted.

Oscar met her eyes. "*La Serpiente* is not even in the country."

CHAPTER 29

"So do you trust this doper Orozco?" Gordon asked.

"I never trust a doper," Selena answered from under the Charger's yawning hood, "but this wasn't the doper in him talking. It was Oscar scared spitless. Say, can you hand me that screwdriver?"

"I still don't get why you didn't arrest him and call for backup. We could have taken him in for questioning and his own protection."

"I was too shocked. Before I knew it, he was back in the cab, hit the gas, and nearly ran me over."

"I put out an APB on him as soon as you called with the description," Gordon said. "Staties will probably find him on the highway headed back to Chicago. Unless he's headed the other way, back to Mexico, maybe, huh? Like The Snake? You believe that?"

"Thousands sneak into America. He can sneak out. He doesn't even have to *sneak* out. You know as well as I do how easy it is to drive across the border southbound. And if he's stopped, there are a few border-patrol agents who will ask for papers, and if they're given two with Ben Franklin's picture, he'll get waved through."

"I'd sure like to confirm whether The Snake is out of the States. Did Oscar say when this was? No? We can check flight manifests for his name and the aliases we know," Gordon said. "Buses, trains, border checkpoint video. That'll eat up a lot of time we don't have."

"Or we can work the Lady Death angle."

"Sure. I'll arrange a warrant for her arrest."

Selena laughed. "I'd like to see you try to serve it. Ah — there it is. You know, it's amazing how just a speck of dirt can block enough fuel or air and make an old car like this run badly. I was worried I'd have to replace the emulsion tube since it was running fine on full throttle. And believe me, it was full throttle."

"You're lucky you didn't wrap yourself around a tree."

"Yeah, well, I'm not next on Lady Death's list," she said lightly, swabbing the rag. "Strange how these guys have all been under the impression that the Aztec goddess of death or *Santa Muerte* or Lady Death has been hunting them."

"So which one is it? We could bring them all in for a lineup."

Selena laughed. *Didn't know he could be funny,* she thought. "The truth is that they all kinda blend together in the minds of Mexicans. I've seen shrines to Saint Death near the cathedral in Mexico City. The Church doesn't like it a bit. But for common folk, it isn't unusual to go in for confession and, on the way out, make a pact with Saint Death. So what Oscar said about The Snake isn't all that farfetched."

"Except the part about Saint Death herself doing the killing."

"Could be someone who likes dressing up as her. It would just take a tunic and a long robe. A globe to indicate her range. And a scythe."

"The murder weapon."

"If we eliminate The Snake, then it is probably someone deeply interested in that cult or in Aztec religion, or both. As I said, they blend easily. I just need to find out more about it. It might show some new connections. Like an engine, you know? Everything fits together."

She ducked out from under the hood, removed the protective cloth from the fender, folded down the rod, and let the hood slam shut.

"Love that sound," she said. "I told you I didn't see those two guys from Miguel's house, didn't I?"

"You did. We're doing neighborhood canvases with the picture, but no one is talking to us in Sandoval's neighborhood so far."

"Not surprised," Selena said. "Can you get a search warrant for her place to find these guys? I'm pretty sure it's her brothers, living with her."

"We can try. It'll have to wait 'til morning. The DA and the judge will have to be in a good mood."

"I called registration at Sinnissippi Community College to check on her flower-arranging class," Selena said. "They won't tell me over the phone if she's in such a class or not. I have to show up in person and flash my shield. I also asked for the names of their anthropology professors. There's one full-timer, Jorge Salazar. We've met before. I'm going to his office hour tomorrow to ask him about Aztec culture and religion. It'll be faster than trying to wade through the million hits I'd get on an Internet search."

"Sounds good," Gordon said. "Hey, look at the time. You want some dinner?"

"I've got some paperwork here at the office to catch up on. Then I've got some shopping to do and some things at home to take care of."

"You feel safe in your house? Need some company? We can order take out."

And have you meet Lorenzo the leech? No way.

"Detective Gordon —"

"Frank. Call me Frank."

"OK. Frank, I can take care of myself. Really," she said, crossing to the counter where she kept the hand-wipes.

"You'll call tomorrow and let me know what you found out?"

"Yeah. I'll call."

"OK. Great. Guess I'll be going." He paused at the door. "You're sure about dinner? I'm buying. There's a new Mexican place down the street. *Dos Amigos*, I think it's called. You could tell me if it's good or not."

"I like Chinese. See you tomorrow."

"Suit yourself." He waved goodbye and left. Selena arched an eyebrow and wondered if she'd just been asked out on a date. *He knows about Reed and me*, she thought. *Strictly professional.* Had to be.

When she got home, Selena found Lorenzo passed out on the couch, snoring. He had finished the Margarita mix, and he had found the Remy Martin cognac she'd bought for Reed. So much for saving that as his Christmas present. The bottle sat uncorked on the end table, inches from Lorenzo's drooling mouth. From the amount left, Selena could tell her brother was going to be out cold for a long time and awaken with a whopper. Selena corked the bottle and set it down far away from his reach. Every light in the house was on. The TV blathered. The sink overflowed with dirty dishes, and the downstairs toilet smelled unflushed. Selena pinched her nose, tapped the handle, and then noticed Lorenzo had sprayed the rim and floor. She wound toilet tissue around her hand to dab it up and flush it away. *Qué una sabandija,* she muttered, *a real slob.*

It wasn't just Lorenzo. None of her brothers ever picked up after themselves, vacuumed, swept, or swished a mop. They never did laundry. They never sliced, diced, chopped, stirred, or poured anything before dinner, and never washed a pan, a dish, or a cup afterward. Never lifted a finger around the house. Selena, of course, had house chores and kitchen duty every day. She was expected to have her bed made and clothes folded and put away. She complained once after scrubbing the floor on her hands and knees with a stiff brush and a bucket of Pine-Sol just before the boys came in and tracked dirt all over it. Mamí squeezed out her sponge, shook a finger at her, and recited the old *dicho,* "*Las mujeres son de la casa, los hombres de la mundo.*" *Women are of the house, men are of the world.*

"That's not fair!" Selena protested. "If you don't make them come back here and clean this up, I will."

Mamí glared at her. "*Las niñas no pelean con los hermanos,*" she rebuked. Little girls don't fight with their brothers — which, taken as a proverb, means that a woman should not compete with men in their world. The first rule of being *Latina* was knowing her place in a man's world.

It was a rule Selena kept forgetting.

She flicked off the light, grabbed a towel, and returned to the living room, where Lorenzo lay drooling. She tucked the towel under his face and wondered how many women he had chased this time before Elena laid down the law. It had always been fine for the boys to date, and they were expected to have two or three girlfriends and to have their way with them. Alley cats. But a *Latina* didn't "date" many boys and would be considered loose, *callejeras*, if she did. A good girl had one *novio* and planned to marry him. For a long time, Selena couldn't understand how her *gringa* friends in high school could date many boys and not be *serio* with any of them.

Her musing was broken by the cricketing of her house phone. She picked it up in the kitchen.

Detective Gordon was on the line. "Sorry to disturb you at home, Selena," he began.

"No, that's OK. What's up?" Was he following up on his dinner offer? Maybe she wouldn't mind getting out, after all.

"You have dinner yet?"

"No. No, actually I haven't."

"The Mexican place wasn't bad. You should have come."

She glanced at Lorenzo on the couch. "Maybe I should have."

"Well, look, I needed to call and tell you the Illinois State Police found Oscar Orozco."

"Good. Where?"

"Wrapped around a tree up near Stillman Junction, not far from Interstate 39. He got himself loaded up on tequila, it looks like, and he lost control of the vehicle. He did not survive the crash."

"Madre de Dios."

"I think you know what this means."

A rattling chill snaked up her back and spread across her shoulders. "I'm next."

CHAPTER 30

Selena found professor Jorge Salazar in the Art Gallery office, standing among open cardboard boxes lined with bubble wrap, examining a headdress of bright feathers.

"Ah, you again, Miss — ?" he opened.

"Selena De La Cruz," she said.

"You came to my office once with some questions about the Aztecs, right? Did the division secretary send you here to get my signature to register for Anthro 103 this spring?"

"I'd like to know if you have a student currently enrolled named Eva Sandoval."

He raised an eyebrow. "Friend of yours?"

"We were going to take the class together."

"Not anymore, I'm afraid. She's already in it this semester. One of my better students. Adult learners usually are. You should know, by the way, that I change the exams every semester so there's no chance of copying."

"You needn't worry about that," Selena said. "Tell me: does the course talk about Aztec human sacrifice?"

"Yes. If you sign up for Anthro 103, we'll cover it there."

"How about a preview?"

"This is hardly the time."

"Just five minutes?"

Salazar's face wrinkled, looking annoyed. "Why is it everyone is so interested in that?"

"It's so — unusual, I guess."

"Not really," Salazar said. "Think about it: Abraham nearly sacrificed Isaac. And Catholics believe Jesus is a human sacrifice as a substitutionary atonement for sins. They re-enact it — or re-present it, as they say — on an altar at every Mass."

"OK, professor, so *you* tell *me* why you're asked about this so often."

"I presume it is the scale. When Cortez showed up, the Aztecs were offering twenty thousand or more human victims each year to the sun god *Huitzilopochtli*. They believed he needed the life-energy of human blood every sundown in order to fight his rivals during the night and emerge victorious in the morning. No blood, no sun. No sun, no life for the people. It seemed logical to them."

"So they yanked out their hearts?"

"Yes. The life force."

"Using a stone knife like the one in your office?"

Salazar paused. "Yes, just like that. It's volcanic glass. It's very sharp."

Selena wondered how she could get it; how to test it in the lab, check for blood samples, DNA. "Twenty thousand a year?" she asked, incredulous.

"Sometimes more, although I think the Spaniards exaggerated the number in order to justify their slaughter and their extermination of the Aztecs' religion. But the number was high. It wasn't done just for the sun god. Every deity in their large pantheon needed appeasing. Their intricate calendar made sure that no deity was offended and that the universe, as a result, would not be destroyed."

"Why would it be?"

"Miss De La Cruz, I'd like to discuss this with you, but I'm very busy here and a bit pressed for time. If you just take Anthro 103 in the spring, we'll cover —"

"Please, professor, that's the last thing, and I'll be on my way." She gave him a disarming smile and flipped her hair. *Do I have to bat my mascara pestañas at you, too?*

"You can look this up online, you know," he said.

"I'm sure you'll be clearer and more correct than Wikipedia," she said. Reed had often complained about students using that source.

He took a quick look at his watch.

"All right," he said, drawing a breath.

To be rid of you, Selena thought.

"The first thing to understand is that the Aztecs had several calendars. The most famous one is the Sun Stone, or the Stone of *Axayacatl,* the one you see in gift shops all over, but it isn't a calendar at all. It depicts the twenty day signs and the four eras of Suns that preceded the Fifth Sun, the final one, but it was not used as a calendar. It was used as a sacrificial altar. I think it's a little funny that you get all these American *touristas* hanging human-sacrifice altars on their living room walls when they get home."

He chortled, but Selena did not join him.

"It's this poster behind me," he went on, pointing to the wall. "Look. Here you see Four of the Five Ages of Man depicted on it and various signs of nature — a storm and a jaguar, for example — that ended each previous age. The Aztecs believed they were in the fifth age, and that the end of the world would begin as soon as their white-skinned god *Quetzalcoatl* returned from his exile across the sea. That's when Cortez showed up and they believed it was The Second Coming of *Quetzalcoatl.* It wasn't."

"But it was, for them, the end of the world."

"Yes, it was. A great civilization was wiped out. Their art, agriculture, architecture, mathematics, and astronomy were well-advanced."

It's what his student Alicia had said. Selena had tapped into one of Salazar's lectures, it seemed.

"That brings us back to calendars," the professor continued. "One calendar, called the *xiuhpohualli,* had 365 solar days. It was related to the agricultural year — quite similar to our own. It was not as important as the *tonalpohualli,* or the sacred day-count. If you calculated the days wrong, it meant the end of the universe."

"How so?"

Salazar lifted his hands palms-up to imitate a weighing scale. "In the Aztec mind, the universe exists in a delicate balance. Divine forces are constantly competing for power. The stand-off is in constant peril of being disturbed by shifting powers of the gods and the natural forces they control. The struggle cannot be won by any one god and never ends. So the world is always at the edge of going under in a spiritual war of gods competing for supremacy. To prevent this from happening, the gods have been given their own space and their own time to rule over. This keeps them apart. The *tonalpohualli* defines how time is divided among the gods."

"How do they know what day belongs to them?"

"It's a complex system." He circled his palms in the air. "Imagine two wheels connected to one another. One wheel has the numbers one to thirteen written on it. The second wheel has twenty symbols on it. In the beginning of the cycle, number one combines with the first symbol. This is the first day of the *tonalpohualli*. The wheels start to move, and number two combines with the second symbol. This is the second day. After fourteen days, an Aztec week of thirteen days has passed. It's called a *trecena* in Spanish. The wheel with the numbers shows number one again. The other wheel now shows the fourteenth symbol."

"Why thirteen days?"

"It's nights, actually. It's a lunar cycle based on new moons. After 260 days, the two wheels have returned to their initial position. The *tonalpohualli* starts all over again. That is, if the gods assigned to each *trecena* have been properly appeased."

"By sacrifices."

"Right. Usually human sacrifices. On the night of the new moon, when the *trecena* begins."

The killings were every thirteen or fourteen days. *Is the killer following an Aztec calendar?* She had to check a calendar and find out —

"When is the next new moon?" she wondered out loud.

Salazar shrugged. "I really don't keep track of it," he said. "Who does, except for weather forecasters and astrologers? But just about any wall or desk calendar will tell you. There should be one in this office. Here — on the wall."

He traced a finger over the spiral-bound calendar tacked above the desk. "Here we go," he said, tapping it. "It's in two days. The eve of the Feast of Our Lady of Guadalupe."

"Is this the one you want, Joe?" called a woman's voice from the gallery storage room.

Alicia emerged from the doorway, draped in a flowing floor-length mantle, cyan-colored with a scattering of golden stars. The closet's fluorescent light, reflecting off the girl's blue-tinted hair, turned her face turquoise.

Selena stood still as stone.

Alicia noted Selena's stare. "It's for the River Falls High School Ballet Folklorico," the girl explained, shrugging off the cape. She began folding it. "The students perform in native costume during the Mass for the Feast of Our Lady of Guadalupe in local churches. I teach them the old dances. It's my final project for class."

"You make a striking *Virgen de Guadalupe*," Selena managed.

"Oh, no," Alicia objected with a dismissive wave of her hand, metallic-blue nail polish sparkling. "This is the mantle of Xochiquetzal, the goddess of life and death."

"Of course, it could also be for The Virgin of Guadalupe," Salazar added hastily. "Did you have any more questions? We have packing to do."

I have a lot of questions, señor professor, Selena thought. "No. Thank you for your time."

She spun on her heel and left, feeling Alicia's daggered stare in her back.

CHAPTER 31

Forty-eight hours.

Selena made her way briskly to the college library, bypassing the registration and records office. Salazar had confirmed Eva's story about her enrollment. But more than that: had she just seen The Blue Lady? The spangled mantle, the azure cast on the skin of the dark-haired girl with an Aztec fascination. Then there was that obsidian knife in Salazar's office. Selena shook her dazed head. Should she ask Gordon to bring Alicia in for questioning? Order a tail?

Forty-eight hours.

At a computer carrel, her mind spinning, Selena searched for "Aztecs" and then found the books in the stacks. She grabbed an armful, spread them on a study table and opened the oversized illustrated volume on Aztec deities.

It didn't take long to notice the snakes.

Feathered Serpent heads covered the Temple of *Quetzalcoatl* in Teotihuacan. Other serpent deities abounded in sculptures: crested rattlesnakes, coiled vipers, and fearsome human figures adorned in snakes, most notably *Coatlicue*. Selena read the caption below her image, depicting her in a skirt of rattlers and a necklace of hearts and skulls:

> After Coatlicue, the Earth Mother of life and death, had given birth to the four hundred ancient star gods, she took a vow of chastity. But one day, while sweeping her shrine at the top of her mountain, a ball of eagle feathers flew up under her skirt of snakes and impregnated her. Her children were angry, thinking that she'd violated her sacred vow not to have any

more children. The divine princess Coyolxauhqui rallied her siblings to kill their mother for this shameful act. But the fetus, the yet-unborn Huizilopochtli, hearing their approach, sprang out fully armed and hacked apart Coyolxauhqui. He threw her head into the sky, where it became the moon. He chased the others into the night sky to be with her. Every morning, then, the rising sun of Huiztilopochtli forces the defeated moon and stars into retreat. But to do this, he must be nourished at sunset for the overnight journey through the dark underworld with hearts cut from the bodies of living men.

Selena's pulse throbbed and her temples drummed. Snake bites. The missing heart. That's what was happening, all right. And if the lunar dates checked out, too, there was no question about it. The killer was appeasing Aztec deities, using The Snake's hit list to cover his or her identity. What else could it be? But how could Alicia know anything about *La Serpiente*?

She flipped a few more pages, fingers trembling. The Mother goddess's name, *Coatlicue*, meant "skirt of snakes," and she was also called *Cihua-coatl*, "lady of the serpent." The ancient snake worship had something to do with fertility and renewal, since snakes shed their skins. A sidebar noted the Mexican national flag, with an eagle and a snake, depicting an Aztec legend of the founding of their great capital after a time of wandering.

She'd seen enough. She dumped the books in a metal return bin and rushed out to the Charger, punching numbers into her cell phone, her black Fitzwell Norah boot heels stabbing the pavement.

"Detective Gordon, please. I'll wait."

She steadied her hand. Bit her lip. She hadn't felt this way since The Snake, suspecting a ruse, had commanded her to kick off her Espadrilles in those smelly slaughterhouse barracks.

"Gordon here," the phone crackled.

"Hello? Frank? I'm on my way in to the station. Do you have a calendar there that shows phases of the moon? Find one and check the dates for new moons against the dates of the killings. I'll be there in a few minutes. Oh, did you get the warrant to search Eva Sandoval's place? Not yet? Soon? How about a tactical team? Good. OK, see you in a few."

CHAPTER 32

Entry unit is ready to apprehend the targets.

We've got intel that someone is in the house.

What's next door? Could be an escape route.

We have uniformed backup ready to provide perimeter control. Over.

Be sure the raid commander has a copy of the warrant.

Copy that.

We have cover units ready in case they break away from the apprehending unit.

Everyone get a good look at the target's mug shot?

Everyone take a good look at one another, too. Don't want to be harming our own.

That's a big 10-4.

County Sheriff's Department will manage custody and handling of prisoners.

I hope there's no dogs. Hate dogs.

I didn't see or hear any when I was there, guys.

Thanks, Selena. Remember, everyone, female suspects go to Selena for a search.

There might be a little girl in the house. Be careful.

Everyone have a cap? We all need a cap for instant ID.

Do we have a high-pursuit vehicle on hand in case of a breakout?

We'll use Selena's. That OK with you, Selena?

As long as I'm driving it.

Funny how those new-moon dates lined up, huh?

River Falls Rescue Unit has been notified to stand by.

Who's got the bolt cutters?

Dress up, everyone. It's showtime.

Selena tugged the helmet chin strap snug and shifted in the Kevlar vest. It didn't fit well, a problem when you're not using your own unit's gear. The blue jacket with POLICE in white capitals across the back wasn't exactly her size, either — men's medium. The body armor filled it out. At least she had her own sidearm. *Six rounds left. Probably should get a spare magazine*, she thought. What unsettled her more was the prospect of busting into a house where Jacinta might be. She even looked a bit like the other girl, about the same age. Selena could still hear the thumping boots, the shouts, the ear-splitting blast of her gun, and the pitiful shriek when she —

OK, Alpha Team, go in.

Police! Search Warrant! Open the door!

BAMBAM.

We're in.

No one here.

Clear!

Clear!

It's all clear.

It's a negative.

OK, conduct a search for anything identifying the two suspects.

Selena secured her firearm, removed her helmet, leaned against a door frame, and mopped her brow with her sleeve. She breathed evenly, counting out loud quietly, slowing her racing heart. She tugged off her leather gloves, wiped her damp palms, and pulled on the blue latex gloves for a search.

Like many Mexican homes, the place was full of candles to burn for every imaginable saint and *la Divina Providencia*. Crochet doilies lay on every surface, and the furniture was covered in transparent plastic. The end tables were cluttered with *santo* figurines, and as she'd noticed before, there were several clear cut-glass vases full of freshly cut flowers indigenous to Mexico.

Selena wandered into the kitchen, where she discovered a work area meant for floral work, with a butcher block and a pegboard festooned with gardening tools: stem cutters, pruning knives, a thorn stripper, scissors of all sorts, and wire cutters. Floral clay, foam, ribbons, and tape for arrangements were stored on a shelf. Empty vases and jars filled a wood box in the corner. The area was lit by a Carmen Miranda lamp with gold fringe on the shade. A pair of work gloves lay on top of a latex glove dispenser. Selena opened the fridge. The shelves were rearranged to accommodate vases of flowers.

Detective Gordon leaned into the room. "Anything interesting here?"

"Eva Sandoval is serious about her flower-arranging class, that's for sure," Selena replied. "What's upstairs?"

"Bedrooms. One has lots of stuff suggesting two men are occupying it. Could be our suspects. There's a fingerprint team working the room and the upstairs bath. There's a room with little-girl stuff. Must be for Jacinta when she's here. Care to see it?"

She nodded, although her heart skittered with apprehension. What if she were here, in the closet hiding, as with the other girl? *Get serious*, she told herself. *It's not going to happen twice.*

She followed Gordon up the stairwell and peered into the room. She stepped inside, and it was like stepping into a dream. Suddenly the room looked foggy, as though a mist had drifted into it. The plain metal-frame bed looked rumpled, with pilled blankets and a navy-blue rib cord spread. The pillows looked disheveled, stuffed bears and bunnies scattered on the braid rug on the plank floor, and the radio on the bedside table looked oddly angled. A framed print of Our Lady of Guadalupe hung over the bed, the Blessed Mother's gentle gaze turned to the closet with the Hannah Montana poster on it.

Madre de Dios, she prayed, *don't let it happen again.*

Selena padded to the closet. Reached for her pistol and thought better of it. Flung open the door.

Metal hangers clinked. A few dresses swished. T-shirts swayed. *Brown Is Beautiful*, one said.

Selena sighed in relief.

But where could the little girl be?

Officers passed Selena in the hallway, bearing cardboard boxes full of items to examine more closely in the county lab. *'Scuse me. Look out. Comin' through. Thanks.*

Selena turned to Gordon. "What now? Find Eva Sandoval and take her in for questioning?"

"Do you really think she'll talk to us if she wouldn't talk to you?"

"Good point."

"Besides, I've got plenty on my plate. This isn't the only show in town, you know. In a small town, we handle everything. I've got a livestock theft case, ammonia chloride missing from a barn that makes me think meth lab, accident reports, a complaint about barking dogs and another about trash dumped on a farmer's field. There have been a few burglaries. You know, people in the country are so trusting, know their neighbors and don't lock their doors. Anyway, never a dull moment, huh? I've got to get back to the station. This is in the County Sheriff's hands now."

"What'll I do?"

"Selena, if you really are next on the list and if the killer is sticking to the lunar schedule, we have about thirty-six hours to figure things out."

And put some things in order, Selena thought. *Just in case.*

"I'll call you if anything comes up. Keep your phone turned on. C'mon, let's go."

He guided her out with a hand on her shoulder. It was strangely comforting.

At the front door, they heard murmurs and catcalls. A crowd had gathered in the street. Uniformed officers ordered people to stand back and make way. Men shook their fists, and women called out insults. When they saw Selena, a few spat and one called out *"¡Traidora! ¡Pocha! Is this how you treat your own people?"*

"Never mind them, Selena," Gordon said. "Get in the cruiser with me, and I'll take you to the lot where you parked."

"Thanks." But getting in a car with a white cop was surely a sign of a *renegada*, a sellout.

"Good thing you didn't park here," Gordon added, cranking the engine and flipping on his roof lightbar. "You might have gotten a few dents in that gorgeous car of yours."

CHAPTER 33

Family of Chicago Girl Wounded in Police Raid Sues

Chicago — The family of a 12-year-old girl seriously injured by a DEA Special Agent's bullet during a raid on their South Side home filed federal and state lawsuits Monday against the DEA and Chicago Police Department, claiming the female shooter and other officers knew there were children in the house but burst into the home with guns at the ready anyway.

Stanley Wiggins, the attorney for the family of the injured girl, Alexis Santa-Ana Jose, said DEA officials and city police had no legitimate reason to smash in the front door and throw a flash grenade into the home of Miss Santa-Ana Jose early Saturday.

Wiggins noted that police and DEA officers, who acted on the hearsay of a paid confidential informant, kept the house under surveillance for several hours before calling in a tactical team.

"They just had to know there were children living in that house," Wiggins stated at a press conference in his office in the northwest Chicago suburb of Hoffman Estates. Wiggins said there were two children in the home, Alexis, age 12, and a male cousin, age 14.

The front yard was scattered with toys and juvenile sports gear, including a Huffy Disney Princess girl's bike.

"Don't tell me that after a few hours of surveillance, they didn't see that stuff, and didn't conclude there were minors in the home," Wiggins said.

The federal lawsuit claims that police and DEA officials violated Alexis Santa-Ana Jose's constitutional rights and seeks an unspecified cash recovery of more than $100,000.

A four-count lawsuit filed in Illinois State Court seeks damages of more than $50,000 for each count. The final amounts that the family will claim in both suits will likely rise much higher.

Wiggins said a civil suit against the female shooter was under consideration.

A DEA spokesman said officers served a legitimate search warrant for both the upstairs and downstairs of the duplex. Officers threw the so-called "flash-bang" grenade into the downstairs quarters early Saturday morning when no one responded to officers' knocking. The spokesman acknowledged that a female Special Agent's gun discharged, wounding the girl, after a bedroom confrontation.

The 14-year-old cousin, whose name is being withheld, was arrested and charged with possession of cannabis and drug paraphernalia.

The tactical team was accompanied by a camera crew for Crime Time TV's program "Busted." An executive with the cable channel said the camera crew did not enter the house with the officers but remained outdoors.

The video reportedly shows DEA and Chicago police officers bursting into the home with weapons drawn. The video also contains the barking of the family dog and sounds of two shots that allegedly killed the dog. The crew recorded footage of the female shooter carrying the wounded girl out to awaiting paramedics. The camera operators turned over their recordings to authorities.

Wiggins denied a request by news organizations, including this newspaper, to review the video. Wiggins said that city police and the DEA are trying to cover up the true details of the raid.

The Chicago Police Department asked the Cook County Prosecutor's Office on Monday for an independent investigation of the shooting. County Prosecutor Jason Ford said he asked the Illinois State Police to lead the investigation.

The DEA spokesman said they would also conduct an internal investigation, according to their policy whenever a firearm is discharged in the line of duty.

The female Special Agent, whose name is being withheld, has been placed on indefinite Administrative Leave pending the investigation.

Selena sighed and planted the tip of the ballpoint pen on the bottom of the photocopied article. It was one of several she could have sent. She'd saved clippings from *The Chicago Tribune, The Sun-Times, USA Today, The Wall Street Journal, Time.*

Dear Reed [she wrote], *The female agent was me. I can't NOT tell you any longer. This case and another — much more serious — have come back and have required my full attention. I had hoped to put all of this behind me. Please forgive me and understand that I could not have you nearby until these matters were resolved. By the time you receive this, it will be over, and you'll be contacted.*

But maybe not by me, she thought, her heart breaking — depending on the outcome.

She lifted the pen. It hovered over the page. How to sign it? His notes ended with *Fondly, Reed* or *Tenderly, Reed* and even *With affection, Reed.* Always the gentleman.

Dare she say it?

She bit her lower lip. She couldn't live with regrets anymore.

She pressed the pen into the paper.

With my love, your Selena.

The doorbell chimed. Lorenzo called from downstairs. "Pizza guy's here. How do I pay him?"

"Be right there," she called back. She folded the letter, stuffed it into the pre-addressed stamped envelope and sealed it. It would go in the mail on her way out of town.

"Hey, hurry up, sis! The guy's waiting."

She hustled down the stairs and shoved some greenbacks into the delivery boy's outstretched hand. He counted them, muttered, "Thanks," and left.

"We're leaving after dinner so be ready to pack up your stuff," Selena informed her brother, shutting the door.

"Leaving? For where? And what's the hurry?"

"I'm going to *Madrina's* for the Feast of Our Lady of Guadalupe."

Lorenzo set down the pizza box and opened it. "Since when did you get so religious?"

"I go every year. You know that. Just eat, will you?"

"What, no grace?" he asked, sarcastic.

"I said eat."

"And what do you mean, 'we'? Why should I go?"

"I told you this isn't a good time for you to be here."

"It's a great time. The place is empty. I can look after it for you while you're gone."

She almost spat out her food. "Yeah, right. I'm dropping you off at Francisco's. He already agreed."

"How much did he ask you to loan him?"

"What's it to you?"

"A hundred, right?"

She waved her pizza slice. "Mind your own business."

"You seem kinda nervous."

"You seem kinda nosy."

"It's those poker games we played when we were kids, don'tcha think?" he said, his mouth full. "He got carried away with it. Started betting his lunch money at school."

She ignored him. "I already called *Madrina*, and she's expecting me in a couple of hours," she said. "You know she'll also expect you boys to show up for the *Mariachi* Mass with roses. Don't disappoint her."

Lorenzo snapped open a cola. "Why are you in such a hurry? We can drive up tomorrow after a good night's sleep."

"I just need to see her, OK?"

"Lemme guess: is this guy Reed bothering you? I'll take care of him."

"Grow up. I don't need brothers to take care of me. I can take care of myself."

He laughed and some wet dough tumbled from his mouth. As with many Mexican men, the idea of an independent *Latina* was a contradiction in terms to him.

"OK, I'm done." Selena reached for a napkin.

"Just one slice? You gonna finish your crust?"

He grabbed it before she could answer.

"We're leaving in thirty minutes, Lorenzo."

"That's not enough time to finish."

"We'll take the rest in the car."

"Can we pick up some beer on the way?"

"What do you think?"

The Beast was too loud for conversation, and Lorenzo was bopping with his eyes closed to a Latin rapper on his iPod. So Selena took the time to remember the first time she met The Snake.

It was this time of year, the holiday season, near *La Fiesta del Nuestra Señora de Guadalupe,* when the staff at the downtown Chicago FBI and DEA offices got together for a dinner out, a dress-up affair intended to remind everyone that they didn't just occupy the same building a few floors apart but were on the same side. The brass told everyone to mingle a bit, even if the G-men thought of DEA as gun-happy Cocaine Cowboys and Drug Enforcement thought of them as suits.

Barely six months out of the Academy, Selena sat at a round table with other women from the Money Laundering Unit, checking her silver Seiko wristwatch way too often. Some guy from Accounting sat next to her, trying to pick her up. His deodorant had given up hours ago. There were damp circles under his arms.

He bit into a tortilla chip and grinned, chipotle mashed between his caps. "Hey, Selena, have you tried this dip? It's spicy, like you."

Selena sipped from her glass of ice water and thought about splashing him in the face with it. "Sorry, I haven't," she said. Feeling warmer than before, she shrugged out of her black Ann Taylor jacket and hung it on the chair's back.

"Heck of a holiday party, huh?" the man said, chewing, looking around the hotel ballroom. "Must have cost a pretty penny to rent this joint."

Spoken like an accountant, Selena thought. She tugged absently on her silver hoop earring and glimpsed the man's name tag. *Hi, I'm Andy.* Across the table, beyond the poinsettia centerpiece, two male Special Agents flirted with female clerks from the Financial Investigation Unit.

"They prob'ly used the cash our guys took in the Aurora bust last week," Andy said. "How much was it?"

"Quarter mil, I heard," Selena said with a pout, turning to the kitchen doors, where *Latina* servers in sharply pressed black-and-white uniforms emerged with salad bowls clicking on platters. Some of them probably commuted from those Aurora neighborhoods, Selena mused. *Huge Mexican presence there. Bigger than the Pilsen neighborhood, where I grew up.*

She sighed, peeved that she hadn't been asked along on the Aurora op. Didn't she score as high as any man on the exams, run the firearms range in two and a half minutes with eighty-five percent of her fifty rounds in the target's red kill zone, and scare the living daylights out of her male classmates on the high-speed chase track?

But they had parked her at a desk from Day One to answer phones and file the Money Trail Initiative Reports submitted by the Special Ops Division. They said it was to make the best use of her business degree from Loyola that her *Papá* insisted she earn. But she had heard the snickers: *Chicks are too soft to pull the trigger.*

You do *know the real reason you're here at all, don't you?* Agnes Bloomberg, the office gossip, confided to her behind her knuckles. *Di-ver-si-ty, honey. They needed to report more female and Hispanic recruitment. They got to check off two boxes with you.*

That night, Selena had told her *Mamí* in tears, "I think I might quit. I didn't join up to sit at a desk all day."

"What did I tell you, *mija*," her mother said, shaking a dish towel at her. "That is no place for a woman. Here, scrape these for me so I can wash them."

Selena slid a spatula across the plates with the leftover flan. "I trained hard to be in the street. Where the action is."

"That is no way to find a husband," her mother scolded. "*¿Qué dirá la gente?*" What will people say?

"Who cares what they'll say?"

"They'll say *qué pasa?* A good-looking *mujer* like you, out of college and still no husband?"

"I have a career to build."

"Maybe it is good you are at a desk, inside, out of the sun. You're dark enough. Outside, your nose will cast a shadow like a sundial. Then what man will have you? That is good enough, *pequeña hija.* Give me the plates."

A waitress dropped a plate of chopped iceberg lettuce and tomatoes in front of her.

"Salads?" Andy spat. "That's girly food. Where's the meat?"

"Excuse me," Selena said, bunching her napkin and throwing it on the table.

"Hey, aren'tcha hungry?"

She didn't answer. She grasped her clutch purse and weaved around tables toward the cash bar. On the way, a seated silver-haired woman in ruffles grabbed her arm.

"Pardon me, miss," she said, wiggling a mug, "but when you get the time, could you bring me more coffee?"

Selena pulled away without a word.

"Maybe she doesn't speak English . . ." a voice behind her trailed.

She stood in a short line at the bar, arms crossed, tapping her black patent leather Sergio Rossis. She made a face. *Could you bring me more coffee?* she mouthed. *The nerve.*

"What was that, miss?" asked the *Latino* barkeep.

"A screwdriver, *por favor, y va fácil en el hielo porque duele los dientes.*"

"Ho-kay, not much ice," he said. The pinched lips and the glint in his eye said *you're not really one of us.* He reached down for a glass and muttered *pocha.*

"What was that?" she fired back.

"Six dollar, please."

"*Míreme*, look me in the eye. That's not what you said." It was an insult, as bad as *agringada*, so Americanized, no longer truly *Mexicana*, a sellout.

"Six dollar," he repeated.

"This one's on me," came a man's voice from behind her. A ten-spot flapped at her earring.

She brushed it away. "I'm in no mood, Mister —"

"Bragg."

The blood rushed to her face. It was the Special Ops Unit supervisor, Del Bragg.

"Mr. Bragg," she blurted out, startled. "What a surprise."

"Call me Del," he said. "We're not at the Academy anymore. Listen up: I need a date."

She poked out her lower lip. "A date? You're asking me out? Are you kidding?"

"Not like that," he said. "C'mere." He stuffed the greenback in the barkeep's jar, took her elbow and guided her out of the man's earshot. "My team has been working up a food chain, and the last guy we flipped to become a CI introduced me to his distributor, who's having a major house party tonight. We hear it's gonna be big. He's spreading a rumor that I have a cartel connection. He told me to show up with a date."

"Since when do dopers ask their guests to come with a squeeze?"

"This is upscale, Selena. The party is in a penthouse. I rented this monkey-suit for *that* party, not this one."

Selena gave his tux the once-over. The crisp bow tie looked like a double exclamation point under his Adam's apple. Then it hit her. "You mean this is for right *now*?"

"What do you say?" Bragg said. "I've cleared it from above. You won't even have to change clothes. You look sharp. Only one thing I ask."

Her heart was hammering. "Sure. What's that?"

"Let me do all the talking, all right? Act dumb."

"You mean, like I can't speak?"

He drew his finger across his lips like a zipper. "Not a peep. Silencioso."

It was almost funny. He meant *callado*. She pursed her lips. "You want me to smack bubble gum, too?"

"C'mon, Selena. The less you know and the less talking you do, the more likely we won't blow the cover. I'll brief you on the way over. For starters, your new name is Selena Peña. I'm Juan Rivera."

She giggled. "You don't even look Latino."

"Neither does Geraldo Rivera," he retorted. "It's a name I can remember. For Johnny Rivers, the old rock'n'roller?"

"Didn't know he was Latino. Maybe you should have chosen Ricky Martin."

"Funny. Anyway, just be sure to call me by that name if you have to call me at all."

"Got it. Is the rest of your street team our surveillance backup?"

"It's just us."

"You're kidding."

"I don't kid about stuff like this. You know, in a case like this, any backup team is just an ambulance with the engine running. We'll be long gone if something goes wrong. Still up for it?"

Selena stepped back to the barkeep, seized the screwdriver glass from the countertop, and drained it. Plunked the glass down hard. The ice rattled. "I'm ready."

The sunglassed *hombres* in the lobby checked their IDs and patted them for weapons before they stepped into the elevator. Bragg had already advised her to be silent in the cab on the way up to the penthouse, suspecting bugs. When the doors *shooshed* open, a uniformed attendant exchanged their coats for numbered tags as a waiter greeted them with a silver tray of seltzer drinks. They plucked two glasses with lemon slices and parsley sprigs. Selena gripped hers tightly enough to avoid any nervous clink of ice cubes. Bragg offered his arm with a reassuring smile. Selena took it. They strode into the window-lined room, Chicago's Loop ablaze all around them.

A live band with accordions and *norteño* guitars pumped a polka-like *narcocorrido*, the lyrics glamorizing the drug lords of northern Mexico. The air was scented with brandy and Havanas. It was probably the strongest narcotic on the premises — besides the palpable pheromone of power.

A barrel-chested man with his oiled hair slicked straight back peeled away from a conversation and approached them. He smoothed his toothbrush mustache and looked like the kind of man who blew kisses to his reflection.

"Señor Rivera," he crooned, extending a beefy hand. "So glad you could come." He bowed to Selena. "Carlos DeMaría, at your service, *señorita*," he said.

She offered her hand to be kissed. Like a gentleman, he barely cupped her hand in his and he did not touch his puckered lips to her knuckles.

"May I introduce Selena Peña," Bragg said.

"Delighted," DeMaría said, looking her down and up with stops each way. "*Dígame acerca de usted mismo, señorita.*" Tell me about yourself.

Selena fluttered her eyelashes. "*Tantas curvas y yo sin frenos.*"

DeMaría laughed and patted her hand. "Ho ho, that's a good one," he said. "I haven't heard that *piropos* in years." He winked at Bragg. "*Ay*, this one has spirit. I approve. Come, Mr. Rivera, there are people I want you to meet."

"One moment," Bragg said, stepping back. He cupped his mouth to Selena's ear. "What did you tell him?"

She whispered back: "So many curves, and I have no brakes."

"Don't overdo it," he said. "Could you please just hang out by the bar and try not to get in trouble?"

She pecked him on the cheek. "You say the sweetest things, *cielito*."

DeMaría steered Bragg away. "Where did you find her . . ." he asked, the voice melting into the band music.

I found her in the Financial Tracing Unit, where she's been tracking your asset-transfers to Mexico, where else, dopehead? Selena murmured to herself on the way to bar. Glasses of red and white were already poured and lined up for taking. She chose a red.

A thin man in a shiny suit stepped to the bar and snatched a white. The cleats on his rattlesnake-skin boots clicked on the hardwood. He wore a shadow of a beard and looked like he needed a solid meal, not another glass of wine. He probably used as much meth as he sold, Selena thought.

"A woman such as you, alone on such an evening?" he said, standing too close.

"I'm with Bragg," she said in self-defense, and immediately her heart clutched.

"Bragg?" the man asked, tilting his head. "Who is that?"

"Rivera," she corrected herself. "Juan Rivera. Over there."

"Yes," the man laughed. It sounded like a hiss. "As though that is his real name. But we all have many names in this business, *no*? What is yours, *señorita*?"

"Selena."

"And tell me, Selena," he said, stepping closer, *jalapeños* on his breath, "why did you call him by the other name — Bragg?"

"Because he is arrogant," Selena said, waving a dismissive hand, "full of himself. A man who does not know his place. It is my nickname for him."

"How is it that you can give him such a name?" the man asked, intrigued. "I am led to believe that he represents The Barracuda's interests here."

"*I* do," she said. "He is my associate, not the other way around."

"Then why aren't you over there?" He pointed to the knot of men in Armani tuxes.

"Because I am a woman, and you know what they would say about a woman knowing her place. *Las mujeras son de la casa, los hombres de la mundo.*"

He raised his glass as though toasting her. "I, for one," he replied gallantly, "have never believed that a woman's only place was in the home."

"*Gracias,*" she said. "I should ask you the same question, *señor.* Why aren't *you* over there?"

"I am not a big enough fish for their pond," he said. "And as Miguel de Cervantes said, 'Never stand begging for that which you have the power to earn.'"

"What is it you hope to earn?"

He lowered his voice. "The *respeto* of The Barracuda."

"For what reason?"

"You see those men, dividing up the Chicago market? They have no vision. They do not know Downstate is a faster-growing market, so fast, in fact, with so many immigrants in rural areas, that it is in need of a sure supply for distributors I have come to know. With the police closing so many meth labs and the pharmacies locking up ingredients, there is a ready and eager market for imported product."

He was trying to impress her. Was he really in touch with the networks of dealers in central and southern Illinois, perhaps beyond?

"The Barracuda is seeking such a partnership," she said boldly.

"I would be most pleased to discuss it further with you privately," he said.

The band struck up a sultry *Paso Doble.* Couples strode to the room's center.

"If I may have the honor?" the man asked, raising his palm.

They set down their glasses. She pressed her palm to his and they stepped to the dance floor where they kept their hands together. It was a bullfighter's song with a dramatic trumpet flourish announcing the beginning of a match.

"I did not catch your name, *señor,*" she said, taking her position, ready to lead with her heel as *Papá* had taught her for her *Quince.*

He planted his other palm in the small of her back. It was cold. She felt his nails curling through the jacket.

"I am called *La Serpiente,*" he said.

CHAPTER 34

Selena climbed the steps to her *Madrina's* porch, recalling how she had sat here as a child, listening to songs by Francisco Gabilondo Solar, the "Singing Cricket." *Mamí* and *Madrina* had sent her to school down these stairs with *taquitos de frijoles* wrapped in aluminum foil for lunch while the other kids brought peanut butter and jelly or cold-cut sandwiches in metal lunch pails with cute pictures of Disney characters. "La Cucaracha" trilled from a car horn down the block, and Jose Feliciano's *Feliz Navidad* was playing somewhere.

Selena pinched her lips together and fought back a tear. Would this be her last visit?

The door squeaked open behind her, and Comadre María stood there in an apron and kerchief. "I knew it was you, *pequeña hija*," she said with a toothy smile. "That old car — such a racket. You'll wake up all the *niñas* put down for the night."

Selena squeezed her shoulders and kissed both cheeks. "*¿Madrina, como son usted?* You've been well?"

"*Buena*, very well," she replied. "Come in, child, come in."

The parlor smelled of *copal* incense burning for the souls in purgatory, something *Madrina* had left over from the Day of the Dead observances. Vanilla votives flickered everywhere, invoking all her favorite saints. Selena worried about a blind woman burning candles.

In the kitchen, the radio played a 12-stringed guitar *corrido* of Lydia Mendoza, the Lark of the Border. A stainless-steel pot of *habichuelas* was soaking and had been for hours. Selena used canned beans and always felt guilty about it. It was part of the shame of an only daughter who habitually burned the *frijoles*, mixed whites and colors in the wash, and scorched the men's shirts with an iron. Thank God for slow cookers, cold-water detergent, and permanent press.

The tea water whistled, and Comadre María offered chamomile tea, the Mexican medicine for anything that ails you. As usual, she knew something was on Selena's mind.

They sat at the table with their steaming cups. Comadre María took Selena's free hand. "I am so very glad you came a day early," she said warmly. "There is so much work to do. We have to decorate, and clean, *ay*, the cleaning I have left, and shop for our family dinner after Mass tomorrow night."

If it was like last year, the menu included sweet *tamales*, stuffed *chiles*, *chorizo* and cheese cubes, and *peches de la Veracruz* with rice colored in the red, white, and green of the Mexican flag. No doubt *Madrina* would try to haggle the prices in the supermarket, and Selena never had the heart to tell her this wasn't done in the States.

Selena squeezed her hand. "*Madrina*, I am so sorry, but I cannot stay, and that is why I came early," Selena apologized. "Something very important has come up, and I can only stay the night. Please don't be angry with me."

"Angry?" the woman said. "How could I ever be angry with you, *mi pequeña hija*?"

My *Mamí* would have been, Selena thought.

"What is it *La Virgen* herself said to Juan Diego?" *Madrina* remembered. "*'My youngest and dearest, am I not here, your merciful mother? Are you not under my shadow and protection?'*"

The Mother of God wasn't anything like her own mother, Selena realized. If anything, she was like her *Madrina* — *always understanding.*

Madrina patted her hand. "I have something for you, Selena. It is just right for this occasion." She reached into her dress pocket and produced a round tin box. She extended it for Selena to take.

Selena took it and twisted off the lid. With a soft gasp, she lifted out her *Madrina's* rosary, the one with the imprint of Our Lady of Guadalupe on the medallion, a silver papal cross, and scented beads in the shape of roses. The wood beads were well-worn, rubbed smooth in places where Comadre María's faithful hand had passed as she meditated upon the mysteries of redemption.

"I've prayed for you with this every day all these years, asking for Our Lady's protection over you," Comadre María said. "It is time for you to have it."

"*Mi Madrina querida*, I can't —"

"You must. It will be a holy reminder that you must be like *La Virgen de Guadalupe*."

"A virgin? But I am." She'd been afraid of hell and her *familia's* shame and of Papá's wrath, of course, but as a grown woman, she was afraid of losing her independence. *Pure is powerful*, she had told herself, and it was something no man could take from her.

"I don't mean only that," her *Madrina* said with a little laugh. "I mean, as the moon reflects the light of the sun and has no light of its own, she who has the new moon under her feet reflects the light of her Son, claiming no light of her own. It is her joy to do this. See how she dances."

"Dances?"

"Most people see the *tilma* image and think she is bowing in humility and praying with the folded hands, and it could be," Comadre María said, "but I think, if you notice the knee slightly bent and the hands tilted up, she is dipping and clapping an Aztec dance."

"A dance?"

"Who is not joyful when one is in the will of God?" *Madrina* said. "So do not feel badly about leaving tomorrow. It is the will of God. As the *dicho* says, *haz el bien y no mires a quién*. Do what is right, without looking at who is watching."

CHAPTER 35

I am watching your new moon rising, Coatlicue, mother of gods, and the New Age of your reign is ready to begin. Arise, arise, queen of heaven, to your proper place. Rule the night as your divine son rules the day. May the iyolla, the blood's life force, of the virgin I offer you this sacred night stay your anger against your people, and may her pure heart nourish your son for his dark journey so that he, too, will arise to give the earth his own life-giving light. I will send it to you through your favorite child in my collection, the barba amarilla, so that you will receive it whole and undamaged.

May I please Xochiquetzal, the blue princess who gives life and takes it back again. May she strengthen my hand and guide my blade.

I am ready.

First, I'll have to cut the blue dahlias and the white roses.

Only fresh ones will do.

CHAPTER 36

She was driving The Beast at night, cruising at 85 miles an hour, able to see only so far as the headlamps could reach on a dark night of the new moon. A ghostly fog prevented her from using her high beams to see farther ahead. The window was rolled down so she could hear the thunder of the big engine, especially when she gunned it around the curves, feeling the Gs pressing her spine into the seat. She loved the rush of it, the freedom of it. She glanced into the rearview mirror but, like every other time, different scenes were playing there that she couldn't outrace: her drunken *Papá* slapping her into the wall and her *Mamí* helplessly pulling on his other arm, Antonio wasting away from the meth, the riflemen at his burial firing three rapid volleys into the iron clouds, the jeers from the Academy men when she nearly dislocated her shoulder shooting a 12-gauge shotgun for the first time, the flash-bang, the trampling boots, the flung door, the ear-splitting report of the Sig Sauer and the spinning remote control.

She pressed the accelerator slowly, slowly, and The Beast roared ahead faster, faster, still faster. The wind shrilled like an airliner's jet turbine. She pulled back on the steering wheel, and the front bumper lifted, lifted, until the road disappeared below the broad hood and the back wheels left the pavement with a dinning screech and she aimed for the morning star that looked like a plane coming in to land at Midway. The wind blustered her dark hair, and it waved and snapped behind her like black fire. She soared higher, higher, seeing only clouds in the rearview mirrors now, tumbling behind her, falling away in rolling billows as she flew up, up —

Up, up, Selena. Selena, wake up. Despiértate, mija.

Comadre María shook her shoulder.

She emerged from the dream, dizzy and disoriented.

"Is everything all right?" Selena asked.

"You tell me. You've been tossing and talking all night."

"What did I say?"

"I couldn't make out most of it. Sometimes names. Antonio. Jacinta? And Frank. Is he the man you are seeing?"

"No, *Madrina*, he is a policeman I've been working with."

"So your work is troubling your heart as well. Come. I'll make tea. Would you rather have coffee? How about some *huevos rancheros* for breakfast before you go back?"

"*Gracias, sí, Madrina.*"

"Good," she said, leaving the room and speaking over her shoulder. "Your phone has been making noises since early morning. I'm surprised it didn't awaken you."

Selena threw off the covers and fumbled for her phone. She checked the missed calls, all from a number she didn't recognize. She return-dialed it.

"Father Johnny Sullivan here, *se habla español.*"

"Father, it's me, Selena. You've been trying to reach me all morning? What's the matter?"

"Jacinta had another locution last night. Very unusual. I thought you would want to know what she said."

"I do."

"I wrote it down. Here it is: 'The Lady says *La Serpiente* is ready to strike his enemy, for as the Scripture says,

I will make you enemies of each other:
You, serpent, and the woman.
She will crush your head
And you will strike at her heels.

'*El Diablo* is angry, so very angry, he twists and writhes at the thought of being defeated by a woman. Do not be afraid, *pequeña hija*. I will be with you when you face him. Pray. You must pray.' OK, that's it. Selena? You still there?"

"I'm here."

"What do you think?"

She was perspiring. "I think I need to come to you to make a confession."

CHAPTER 37

For the whole drive back, with The Beast's four-in-one headers and three-inch exhaust pipes bellowing, Selena wrung her mind. She was next in the list. That was certain. Was she really the last? How did the killer find the vics? Or did they always find him first? Why would they go to him willingly if they knew they were marked for assassination? Did they all know? Is it someone impersonating The Snake? Is The Snake really out of the country? Is it a man at all? Is it a woman? The Blue Lady? Is it the one Jacinta sees? Or is it truly *La Virgen*? Is someone acting as Saint Death, *Santa Muerte*? Or an Aztec goddess? Alicia, dressed in that star-studded mantle? Selena shook away the questions as though they were flies, her midnight hair swaying heavily. She engaged the radar detector. No need to get pulled over, even if she had a shield to show.

She reached into her pocket and fingered the loose rosary there, the words to the *Hail Mary* as tangled in her mind as the chain. How could she possibly have forgotten *that*?

She stuffed it back into her pocket.

She pushed the ball of her foot to the floorboards.

And flew.

CHAPTER 38

At St. Mary's church, a crew of Latinos stood on aluminum ladders to fasten red, white, and green bunting in place. Every pew was festooned with paper flowers in the same tricolors, with tricolor ribbons hanging below. A Mexican flag stood beside the American flag on the dais. A life-size painting of *Nuestra Señora de Guadalupe* was propped up in front, to the ambo side of the altar, set in a gorgeous gilded frame that sparkled in the spotlights, like the spiked sunrays blazing behind Mary's royal turquoise cape. *A woman clothed with the sun.* The gold embroidery of her gown glittered like the constellations they portrayed, and the twinkling eight-pointed stars on her mantle reflected the night-sky configuration identical to the date of her appearing to Juan Diego.

At the foot of the frame, vases overflowing with fragrant red roses gathered as though the Queen of Heaven was holding court. Barely visible above the blooms was the little brown angel holding Our Lady's cloak and gown from below, and above him, the smiling curl of the black new moon under her feet.

Long-stem red roses individually wrapped in cellophane for sale later sat in water-filled buckets in the foyer. Selena heard a blare of trumpets and a strum of a *guitarón* from the music room downstairs. The *maríachis* were practicing.

Father Johnny, white as two-percent milk and dressed in a floor-length cassock, directed a knot of brown boys about something. Maybe they were the altar servers. An elderly couple distributed colorful brochures in the pew racks, probably explaining the historical background and customs for *Anglos* who might attend out of curiosity. Selena glanced at her watch. The day was darkening already at five o'clock.

Father Johnny finished his instructions, patted the boys on their heads in dismissing them, and noticed Selena. He ambled up the central aisle to greet her.

She hugged him. "I know you're busy, Father —"

"Never too busy for this. Would you prefer the confessional or my office for a face-to-face? Either is quite secure, I assure you."

"It's been a while, Father. I might feel better in the old-fashioned booth."

"Very well." He ushered her to the oak door near the vestry where two bulbs bulged out from above it, one red, one green.

"Go ahead inside, and I'll be with you in a moment," the cleric said. "I need my stole." He entered the vestry.

Selena knelt in the confessional, a cottony light filtering through a grid in the ceiling. The tightly woven priest's screen in front of her face allowed a faint glimpse of the chair on the other side and a crucifix on the wall beyond it. A laminated card was pinned below the window on her side, titled "Making a Good Confession," with an outline of the procedure and suggested prayers. She unpinned it. She was going to need it.

They called it "the sacrament of reconciliation" these days, and that sounded better. She thought of how angry she'd been at Lorenzo and wondered if they'd ever get along. She thought of all the men she'd been angry with, and, quite oddly, she thought of her middle-school soccer coach when she wanted to join the boys' soccer team. Not that they had a *problema* recruiting boys for the team, as happens in some school districts. And it wasn't because there wasn't a girls' team — there was, and they were pretty good. But growing up with three brothers, she needed more competition. A challenge. So Antonio took her to the boys' field to introduce her to the coach. She politely asked to join the team, bouncing a ball knee to knee to show him what she could do. But the man spat out his whistle and laughed at her. "The cheerleaders are over there," he said, pointing behind her and widening his stance. It sure looked like a goal. So she drop-kicked the ball hard right between his goalposts, so to speak. She was suspended for three days. *Mamí* had the fire of an *amazona* in her eyes when she got home. *"¿Y qué te ha entrado a tí? ¿No te importa el que dirán?"* she scolded while stirring *frijoles* furiously on the stove. *What has gotten into you? Don't you care what people will say?* "They'll *say* I should have been allowed to try out," Selena said, displaying the unbecoming *gringita* habit of speaking her mind. So she was sent to bed without supper as well.

Father Johnny entered his side of the booth, sat, draped the stole around his neck, kissed it, and made a Sign of the Cross, saying, "Whenever you're ready, dear. Do you remember how to begin?"

"Bless me, Father, for I have sinned. It's been, gee, a long time. Father, I'm a little afraid."

"That's no sin. Take your time."

It drained out. The anger, the vengeance, the deceit, the envy, the resentment, the jealousy, all the venom that had poisoned her. When finished, she dabbed her eyes with her sleeve and stumbled through the Act of Reconciliation, reading from the card.

"And what is my penance?" she asked weakly after absolution.

"Say a Hail Mary, do not refuse Our Lady's embrace, and believe in God's healing forgiveness."

"Really? Just one Hail Mary?"

"She's not like so many other mothers, Selena," Father said. "She doesn't nag and needs no nagging to pay attention to you."

"OK, Father. Thank you." She smiled in the darkness.

"And bring Jacinta back to Mass tonight," he added, signaling through the screen to step outside. She did.

"Bring her back?" she asked, forehead furrowed.

"I'm very worried about her," Father Johnny said, folding his stole. "After the locution I told you about, she asked me where poor Miguel was buried so she could go and pray for his soul. Yes, Detective Gordon told me all about that, and I must have mentioned it to her. I said it was at the Pentecostal church cemetery outside town, where one of their ministries is to bury the homeless, God bless them for it. He had no relatives, can you believe it? And then I asked if she would come to Mass tonight and she said she might, after praying in the cemetery, and I blabbed on about how lovely it would be, especially with the Ballet Folklorico coming from the high school in costumes —"

"In Aztec costumes?"

"Yes, by custom, and the community college is lending them authentic apparel from their collection, but I told Jacinta how bad I felt that we couldn't find the Mexican national flower for our church's decorations because you can't buy them anywhere."

"Why not?"

"They can't be shipped. They have to be freshly cut. And Jacinta said her aunt Eva could help because she grew them in her greenhouse at the community college. In fact, the college let her take over an old greenhouse just to grow Mexican flora for a graduation project. So I asked if the aunt would be so kind as to go there tonight and cut some for us and deliver — Selena? Selena, where are you going?"

"Oh, God, oh, God," she said, bursting out the front doors.

CHAPTER 39

The greenhouse was overgrown with vines that looked like veins, the panels were stained yellow like old chicken skin, and a weedy walk led to it. The college's Hort program had built modern greenhouses across the parking lot near the new Science Center with a sprawling turf farm for the golf-course-management students, leaving this one to be swallowed by the prairie. The cobra-head parking-lot lampposts provided just enough light to pick out the path. But with a new moon, the sky was black as jeweler's velvet with a scattering of tiny diamonds.

The greenhouse lights were on, a sickly lime, shimmering through a square metal vent over the door.

Selena held the Sig Sauer high on her chest, finger straight, listening. Just the buzz of fluorescent tubes and the low whirr of a fan.

Would Detective Gordon show up? She'd phoned him on the fast drive over and left a message that she was on the way here. Kept his cell off after duty hours, it seemed. But she couldn't wait.

She pulled open the door. The rusted springs creaked. After she entered and saw the hanging plants and misting pipes overhead, the door clapped shut behind her.

The lights snapped off. The fan click-clicked to a stop.

A clank sounded at the door. A click. The lock snapped.

Selena spun and felt around for the door handle. Her heart leaped into her throat. She'd been lured in and someone had trapped her.

"You won't get out, you know," came a woman's voice through the door. "Go ahead and shoot at the door. You'll just make holes in it. It's a very durable polyurethane plastic. The padlock will hold."

A dull thump sounded against the door.

The woman outside cackled. "And this timber won't budge, so when I leave, you won't get out for sure."

221

Selena felt around for a light switch. "Eva?"

"I heard the car. Hard to miss. Actually, I've been expecting you."

"It's you, isn't it? Killing those men?"

"Parasites," Eva hissed venomously. "Offering them to the divine ones is my honor. It pleases them. It shows our gratitude for their gifts. It cleanses our community from the poison of drugs. You and I, we want the same thing. We might not have been enemies, if it weren't for your cold, callous rich girl's heart. Traitor."

Selena took aim through the plastic panels, looking for Eva Sandoval's shadow. She waved the pistol back and forth, but she couldn't see any outline of her. Eva was right. She couldn't shoot her way out.

"How did you get the names?" Selena called.

"What's it to you? You're about to die."

"Were you lovers? You and *La Serpiente*? Did you promise to kill them for him? Join him in Mexico later?"

Eva laughed hoarsely. "You're stupider than I thought. Duh! No. We weren't lovers. But I visited him in prison to ask how my sister died. I had to know."

"Sister?"

"Rosita. His bodyguard. I know now how she died. You killed her. He told me everything. You shot her five times for taking your shoes. You —"

"I did nothing of the sort!" Selena shouted.

"The body was so badly burned I didn't recognize her and — and —" The rage swelled in Eva's throat. "If not for you, she would not have died!" Her voice dropped lower. "And he said he would go to Mexico and find The Barracuda on his own, without you. Then he listed all the others he would kill if he stayed. I knew then that these — these vermin, *alimañas*, needed to be offered as an appeasement to our ancestral protectors because we have wandered away from them, and they are angry, and we must repent, just as The Blue Maiden says through Jacinta."

"You don't believe it's *La Virgen*?"

"You can believe whatever you want. Jacinta believes it is her — insulting Xochiquetzal, the Blue Princess of Life."

That's why she beats her.

"Why did you put the names in the Book of the Dead?" Selena called out.

"To make the police think that it was *La Serpiente* at fault. It worked."

"And Miguel? You had him killed?"

"He helped to get the others, acting as The Snake, making big promises. He wanted to take over their turf. Ambitious little rat. He outlived his usefulness and had to go. My brothers took care of him, and the police will never find them, even though they turned my place upside down. That Miguel was such an amateur . . ."

Selena let her talk. She felt her way along an aisle, touching wood frames, leaves, metal table legs, searching for another door, a window. The lights from the parking lot, filtered through the dirty green-house panes, cast dark shadows. If only she had a penlight or a light attachment for the gun. She pulled out her cell phone and thumbed it on. A dull glow outlined the plant tables and reflected dimly against glass boxes. The perfume of gladiolas, the rich fragrance of roses and the bitterness of marigolds swelled in her nose. She bumped into a glass case and heard something like a tambourine. She held up the phone.

The brown-spotted rattler coiled behind the glass lunged out, striking the thick glass with a *thunk*. Selena fell on her backside with a cry. The phone bounced away and winked out.

"Ah, you found the Mexican lance head," Eva said. "A very distinct sound, isn't it? The speckled adder is to the left and the red diamond-back rattler to the right. But here's one you'll really like."

Her heart revving, Selena lifted up on her elbows and heard the faint tone of three cell-phone numbers being punched. Immediately, a hinge squeaked at the far end of the greenhouse, followed by the wet plop of something heavy, like a water soaked mop dropping on the concrete floor.

Viper

"Meet *El Diablo*," Eva said. "I haven't fed him for days, and he's really mad. Now, if you'll excuse me, I'll leave so the two of you can get acquainted. I'd stay and enjoy how this all worked out so well, but I have a virgin to sacrifice — *esa mocosa*, the little brat."

CHAPTER 40

Whatever it was, it was big, heavy, smelled like stale urine, and was on the move, sliding, sliding.

Hunting.

Selena hefted up on her haunches and listened carefully. Snakes detect prey by smell, especially sweat and exhaled breath. *They're drawn to fear.* Isn't that what the coroner had said? They cannot hear, but feel vibrations through their skin. Eighth-grade science class.

It had the advantage in the dark.

Perspiring in the hothouse, she stripped off her coat and hurled it over the central table across the room. It rustled some plants and fell with a *floom* on the concrete floor.

The creature slithered that way eagerly, knocking over clay pots stored under the tables, clattering and shattering them. There was a shuffle of cloth, then nothing.

Then a frustrated, furious hiss.

Then sliding, sliding.

Selena held out the Sig Sauer two fisted, head cocked, turning her ear this way and that, trying to discern the reptile's location. *It's probably several feet long,* she thought, *as long as a man, and a single shot won't do.*

Six shots left.

She fought off sudden dizziness, the "startle response" draining the blood from her head, accelerating her heart, numbing her fingers. *Focus. Where is it? Where?*

The muscular serpent plowed through the lower shelves, crashing through pots and plastic bags of fertilizer and potting soil, spilling them. Selena dashed to her left as the snake coiled on the concrete with the sound of leather creaking.

Selena smelled something new, something not fruity, but — celery? Cucumber? It was uncurling its fangs, dripping venom, ready to strike.

She stiffened her arms and fired the Sig *bam bam bam bam.*

Selena felt the whoosh of its head to her left, smelled the reek of its saliva, heard the snap of its powerful jaws. The shocking tremor of the discharge had stunned it and the acrid, peppery gunpowder threw off its aim. The flash of her shots got her a glimpse of her nemesis — a monster black as tar, wide as her thigh, with eyes of stone and fangs long and sharp as stiletto switchblades.

Madre de Dios, she exclaimed, whirling away, scurrying down the aisle.

The dark serpent followed, undulating, flapping, hissing in rage. Selena smelled the venom again. She turned, aimed low and fired.

Click.

The semiautomatic misfired.

No. Not now.

The monster hissed.

Selena felt the rosary pressing into her leg. She rolled, yanked it out and threw it at the lunging snake.

Highlighted in the faint glow from the parking-lot lights, the *barba* caught the rattling chain of beads in its wide jaws and hungrily gulped it down.

And began to writhe.

And curl and coil and spin over and over, hissing and gasping and snapping in its wrath, in its throes, spitting saliva and poison, crashing into tables, knocking over cardboard boxes of tools and seedlings, slapping against the glass vivaria of other snakes, awakening them to sharp hisses of warning, knocking one over with a splintering crash and the sound of clicking castanets.

Selena hitched her breath. *Another snake is loose.*

She slammed her palm against the gun handle to eject the stuck shell and racked the slide to chamber her last round. She vaulted to the top of the room-length table, kicked aside planters and jumped to the other side. She ran to the door.

The *barba* hacked. Hissed.

And followed her. Slithering, sliding.

Selena felt her way to the front door, hitting her head on hanging pots, tripping on a tray of plants. The dim light from the parking lot flickered through the vent over the door. The vent covering looked soft, like a metal mesh furnace filter. A thin sheet of insulating plastic covered it.

Selena tucked the pistol into her belt. She hauled herself onto the tabletop and, with her toes on the edge, leaned forward as far as she could and ripped off the plastic sheeting. Staples peppered the floor. She reached up and grasped the misting pipes overhead. Would they hold her weight? She held on with both hands. She swung once, twice, and a third time to kick out the vent with her heels. *Bam!* It gave a little. She swung again, and it popped open with a bang.

The *barba* had found the rattler. They hissed and chattered at each other, followed by snapping and slapping sounds. Selena jumped to the floor, found footing in the framing of the paned building, clambered up, and pulled herself up and out through the vent. She tumbled to the grass outside, gulping the cold night air.

Jacinta, she thought. *Jacinta. Pequeña hija.*

She's the virgin Eva will sacrifice.

In the cemetery.

She sprinted for the Charger.

CHAPTER 41

Snarling as never before, The Beast filled the night with its deafening roar. Selena ignored the angry honks of cars she flew past. Weave. Dodge. Accelerate. *Go, go faster.* Her ears throbbed with the furious pumping of adrenaline and her stomach knotted with the dread that even with her speed, she might not be in time to find Jacinta in the cemetery before Eva Sandoval did.

Madre de Dios, sweet Mother, help me, she prayed. *Dearest mother, pray for me.*

There was no way to get other help now. She'd left the phone behind in the greenhouse. Even if she had it, there was no way to thumb numbers now, not at a shuddering 110 miles an hour. Even if Frank Gordon had gotten her message, he'd be on the way to the greenhouse, not the cemetery.

She knew exactly where the cemetery was. It was at that countryside Presbyterian church where the Spanish Pentecostals met, where Rodríguez had been found in that grotto. Selena pictured the high razor-wired fence. How would Jacinta get in? Hadn't Gordon mentioned some digging under the chain-link fence, *too small for a man — but not a little girl.*

She thundered down the off-ramp and screeched past the stop sign around the turn, burning rubber. Just a few more miles.

How would Jacinta get out to the cemetery? Someone from that church, most likely. She had quite a loyal following. Or Eva herself was driving her there, pretending to be helpful.

No, please God, not that.

She zoomed by one car to the left and, with an oncoming car, passed the next one on the right, gravel spraying behind her. She surged around the last turn and half-spun to a stop at the cemetery's front gates.

Eva Sandoval stood in the glare of the headlights, on the inside of the chain-link gate. She wrapped a cable around the gate posts and snapped a padlock in place. Selena leaped from the car and drew her gun.

"Open the gate!" she commanded, taking aim.

"What the devil?" Eva said, shading her eyes with her palm. "*You?*"

"Open it!"

"Virgin one, serpent zero," Eva hissed. "I'm about to even the score. You're too late." She slinked into the darkness with a backpack slung over her shoulder.

Selena ran to the entry, tested the cable, and kicked the gate in frustration. A battered lock lay on the ground; Eva must have hacksawed and hammered her way inside. At least Jacinta wasn't with her. Eva was searching for her. Selena had time.

She examined the top of the eight-foot fencing where coiled razor wire glinted, keeping out vandals. There was no way to climb over it.

Selena jammed the gun back in her belt and ran back to the Charger. She slid in, slammed the door shut, and threw the car into reverse. Looking over her shoulder, she screeched backward just far enough for a drag-racing launch, and halted.

"I hate to do this to you, baby," she said.

She strapped herself in tightly. She held down the brake with her left foot while slowly applying the accelerator pedal with the other foot. The Beast's 10,000 RPM tach needle in the round unit arced slowly to the right with an ever-louder roar. She watched the meter rising, rising. She was trying to feel the point where the car would either start to move or start spinning its tires. The big car shook and trembled, but she held down both the brake and accelerator pedals, waiting, watching the RPM needle, picturing the Sinnissippi Drag Strip's Christmas-tree lights reaching the last amber light before the green.

Now.

She released the brake and pushed the gas pedal all the way down. The Beast bellowed and leaped.

In a flash, she crashed through the gates with a deafening shatter. The fence panel ripped from the ground and rode her hood and roof, scraping the spidered windshield. She struck a tombstone with a terrible splintering sound. The passenger window exploded in a rain of glass pebbles. The hood crumpled and the right fender peeled away. She jolted to a head-jarring stop against another monument, where the grill cracked and the radiator burst with a gasp of steam. A wheel bounced away. Glass tinkled. A belt *flap flap flapped*. Smoke roiled from under the wrinkled hood; steam went *ssshhhhh*. A single headlamp still cast a shaft of light into the graveyard. The chassis creaked as though in pain.

Selena raised her rattled head that she'd cushioned on her forearms, released the seat belt, and shouldered open the door. She spilled from the car, ignoring the burning cuts on her right arm. When she tried to stand, her right knee shrieked. She stumbled. Tried to stand again. The knee felt electrocuted, and the shock made her cry out.

Can't let it stop me, she grunted. Smelling gas, she stiffened the leg and limped away from the car, wincing with every step. She'd turned away from the shattered window, and her face was spared from cuts. She shook out glass pebbles from her hair.

She cupped her palm around her mouth. *"¡Jacinta! ¡Jacinta! ¿Dónde estás?"*

The car hissed and popped.

Selena dragged herself a few more excruciating steps, calling for the little girl. No reply. Eva would hear her, too, and know where she was. What if Eva ambushed her from behind a tall tombstone and ripped her throat out? She couldn't run or maneuver, *not with this knee.*

Where was Miguel's grave? Would Jacinta be there? Or the grotto? That made sense. Selena crossed her arms and shivered. Without her coat, she felt the deepening chill of a mid-December night. The Feast of Our Lady of Guadalupe.

Mother of God, help me, she prayed. *Father God, guide me.*

Brittle leaves in a burr oak whispered in the wind, and beyond them, Selena saw a faint glow of amethyst blue. She forced herself toward it, the knee ablaze. She passed a row of markers, military ones, spare and standing at attention, with little Stars and Stripes planted at their bases. *Antonio*, she breathed, *Antonio, I need your help, too. And your saint's namesake, the one who finds lost things.*

Then she spotted her.

Jacinta was kneeling beneath one of the oaks, staring at a wispy shroud of mist in the branches.

"*¡Jacinta! ¡Soy Selena! ¡Míreme! Look at me!*" Selena called, shuffling toward the girl.

The girl stood and faced her. She called out, "Do you see her now? I told you it was her."

A hulking shadow emerged behind the girl and swallowed her. Jacinta screamed.

"She can't help you now," Eva snarled. "And you — stay where you are."

Selena stopped, the knee protesting in agony.

The lone headlamp of her steaming car cast an eerie golden glow, enough to see Eva's blue gown, determined grimace, and the shining hawk-bill pruning blade in her hand.

"Don't you dare come any closer," Eva warned darkly. "And how the devil did you get out?"

"Let the girl go," Selena ordered, desperately trying not to topple.

Jacinta struggled, and Eva squeezed her against her barrel of a chest until the girl yelped.

"Haven't we gone through this before?" Eva said with a raspy laugh. "At the police station?"

Selena drew her Sig Sauer and extended her arm, the flesh aflame with glass cuts. "Let the girl go or I'll shoot."

"Since when do insurance agents carry guns?" Eva said.

"Drug Enforcement officer. Release the girl now and drop the knife or, I swear to God and his holy Mother, I'll blow your head off."

Eva chuckled. "Drug enforcement? So you're back on the job again. Honest, officer, all I have in the bag are flowers."

"I said now."

"Go ahead. In this light, at that distance, chances are you'll hit Jacinta, not me. Is that what you want?"

Just like before. The little girl.

Eva laughed in contempt. "You can shoot me after I offer her to *Coatlicue,* the true mother of gods."

Eva lifted her voice, chanting, *"Gloriosa y Poderosa Coatlicue, Soberana Señora —"*

Jacinta squirmed against Eva's iron grip.

"Miss Selena!" she cried out, the voice high in her throat.

"Final warning!" Selena shouted.

"Like I said before, you're too late."

She raised the knife.

One shot.

Eye on the sight, not the target.

Selena fired.

Jacinta screamed.

Selena's heart climbed into her throat.

Eva stood with the knife in the air.

The knife dropped from her hand.

Eva Sandoval crumpled in a heap.

Not bad, for a girl.

Jacinta tore away and rushed into Selena's arms.

The little girl shook. "Our Lady said she would protect me. She sent you. Did you know she was there?"

Selena looked up at the gnarled tree.

The mist was gone, but beyond the burr branches, stars twinkled as on *La Virgen's* mantle.

"Sí, Jacinta," Selena said softly, embracing the trembling girl. "I knew."

CHAPTER 42

Selena poured two fingers of cognac in the snifter for Reed Stubblefield.

"I hope you like it," she said. "I had another bottle saved for a special occasion like this, but my brother Lorenzo — well, I told you about that already, didn't I?"

"You did," Reed replied with the tender smile that melted her heart.

"I didn't want to wait until Christmas, when you meet my family," she said, taking a seat beside him on her sofa. She leaned the cane beside her, Reed's "Citizen Cane" that he no longer used. The doctor said she might need it for a few more days while the knee sprain healed.

"Are you going to tell your godmother what happened to her rosary?"

"I don't think so. I appreciate how Detective Gordon pulled it out after he found the *barba* and the rattler dead and tied in a knot. He said the chain was stuck in there pretty solid and the crucifix was caught in its mouth like a fish hook. Say, did I tell you about the recording equipment he found there? Seems that Eva was keeping an audio-diary. How creepy is that?"

"Had she gone to trial, those recordings would surely have convicted her."

"That's what Frank said."

"Frank?"

"Just friends," she said, patting his thigh reassuringly. "I don't date cops any more. No need to worry."

"Glad to hear it."

"He is a sweetie, though. Somehow he managed to clean up the rosary for me. I'll have to ask Father Johnny to re-bless it, I think. I know my godmother will ask me about it, and now I can honestly say I keep it with me at all times."

"I'm looking forward to meeting your *Madrina*."

"You know, I think she'd be a fine caretaker for Jacinta," Selena surmised. "I wonder if Catholic Charities will allow me to take her to Chicago to meet her."

"As long as you don't race her up there in the Charger. How long did you say it would take to be fixed?"

"End of May at least," she said with a wistful sigh. "The collision-repair program at the college accepted it as their project car for the semester. Did I tell you that they'll let me do custom work myself? I'm thinking about replacing the 440 V-8 engine with a 525 fuel-injected Hemi topped with a Stage V intake and a pair of modified 600 Holleys. That should boost the horsepower from 450 to around 530, 540. What do you think?"

"I *think* all I can do is change the oil, *maybe*," Reed admitted with a laugh. He raised his glass. "So to you," he toasted. "For all you — and your car — have been through."

"To us," she said. "It wasn't easy for you, either, not knowing what was going on."

They clicked glasses and took a sip.

"This is splendid, thank you," Reed said, swirling the amber drink. "Now tell me: is there anything else I don't know about you that I should know?"

"Yes, lots," she said with an impish grin. "But I'm not telling you just yet. There's a saying in my culture: *No hay que voltear cada piedra para saber que hay escorpiones bajo unas pocas.* You don't need to turn over every rock to know there are scorpions under a few."

"What's that supposed to mean?"

"You've got a lot to learn, *cielito*," she said, winking playfully.

"Then maybe I should think twice about giving you this," he teased, reaching behind the couch.

He lifted a gift bag with red, white, and green ribbon. *"Feliz Navidad,"* he said.

"Oh, we're learning Spanish, too, are we?" she said, pleased, accepting the bag. "And what's this?"

She removed the white tissue and slid out a pair of Stuart Weitzman sling heels in Adobe Serpent. She put her palm to her chest and gasped, mouth agape.

"I — I just don't know what to say," she stammered.

"Try them on, and then I'll say something, and you can tell me if I'm pronouncing it properly."

"All right." She steadied herself with the cane, stood, and flipped off her blue Roxy Lulu flats. Her heart lifted and felt lighter than ever. "How sweet. And appropriate. Where did you find them? My goodness, what did they cost? Oh, I shouldn't ask. I'm sorry. Thank you. I can't believe it. I don't —"

"Just try them on."

"Right." She slipped her left foot into the snake-print heel and then the right. "Wait. Something doesn't feel right. Oh, there's tissue in the toe."

She sat down, removed the shoe, and pulled out a wad of tissue.

"Don't throw that out," Reed said.

"Why not?"

Then she felt something hard in it. She unfolded the paper.

A round brilliant cut diamond, set in the solitaire mounting of a platinum band, sparkled in her palm.

Her heart skipped a beat. She sucked in her breath. She put a hand to her blushing cheeks.

"Selena?"

"Right, I'm sorry, you were going to say something."

He looked her in the eye. "*Te quiero, Selena,*" he said. I love you. "*Cásate conmigo.*" Marry me.

She had a smart reply for everything men said to her, but nothing for this. Was he really asking her to — did he expect her to — well, after all, she *had* signed the letter *with my love, your Selena.* What should she —

"Well?" he said. "Did I say it wrong?"

"Not bad," she said, primping her mouth. "Try rolling the *r* a little more, like this."

She trilled an *r*, sounding like the husky purr of a cat.

He tried it.

"Much better," she applauded. "Now try it again, and hold the *o* a bit longer."

"*Te quierrroooo —*"

She seized his handsome face in her hands and kissed him when he reached the *o.*

She lingered there and kicked off the other shoe.

THE END

EPILOGOMENA

Know for certain, little one, that I am Mother of the True God
through Whom everything lives, Lord of the far and near,
Master of heaven and earth. Do not fear. Are you not in
the hollow of my mantle, in the crossing of my arms?
Do you need anything more?

Neustra Señora de Guadalupe
(from the Nahuatl, Coatl-a-llope,
"she who crushes the snake")

ACKNOWLEDGMENTS

No book is ever really done by one person but by many who contribute something special. *Gracias* first to my supportive and patient wife, Virginia, who put up with my spending so much time with another woman, Selena. *Te amo, B'jinia.* Thanks also to Sophia Institute Press® editor Regina Doman for once again shaping an unruly manuscript into something readable. Thanks go to publisher John Barger for taking another chance on an off-beat mystery. Finally, a special *gracias* to fellow Catholic Writers Guild member and translator Maria Rivera, who reviewed the work-in-progress for cultural accuracy, correct Spanish, and most importantly, choices of shoes for Selena. Surely there are others I ought to include here, and I pray they will forgive this absentminded professor for the omission.

ABOUT THE AUTHOR

A former producer with Wisconsin Public Radio, John teaches journalism and English at Kishwaukee College in northern Illinois. His first novel, *The Throne of Tara* (Crossway, 1990), was a *Christianity Today* Readers Choice Award nominee, and his second historical novel, *Relics* (Thomas Nelson, 1993, 2009) was a Doubleday Book Club Selection. *Bleeder* (Sophia Institute Press, 2009) was his first mystery. His work has appeared in a wide variety of Christian and secular journals, ranging from *The Critic* to *Apocalypse* to the *Rockford Review*. In 1997, he took Honorable Mention in the *Writers Digest* Competition. He holds an MA in Media from Columbia University and an MA in Writing from Illinois State University. A member of The Academy of American Poets and Mystery Writers of America, he is listed in *Contemporary Authors, Who's Who in Entertainment*, and *Who's Who Among America's Teachers*.

John can be reached at jjdesjarlais@johndesjarlais.com or at www.johndesjarlais.com.

About This Book

On the cusp of a new surge of Catholic literary creativity, Sophia Institute Press® presents this book as part of our *Imagio Catholic Fiction* series.

Pope John Paul II wrote that artists are the "image of God the Creator." *Imagio Catholic Fiction* publishes novels whose authors recognize that precious gift and serious responsibility. Both our new titles and classic reprints are grounded in a Catholic sensibility; they present a moral universe in which God is real and active and in which virtue leads to happiness (if not always success) and sin to death. Yet they are not disguised sermons, but rousing and imaginative stories well told, fit for readers young and old alike.

Once not long ago, we enjoyed an abundance of such books, and these provided Catholic families a haven from the nihilism and prurience of the world's corrupted art. Today we have greater need than ever of such a haven, and happily, after a dry time, these books are being rediscovered and added to. We are proud to be heirs of the great tradition of Catholic fiction, and we aim to pass on that tradition — and to make it richer still.

An Invitation

Reader, the book that you hold in your hands was published by Sophia Institute Press.

Sophia Institute seeks to restore man's knowledge of eternal truth, including man's knowledge of his own nature, his relation to other persons, and his relation to God.

Our press fulfills this mission by offering translations, reprints, and new publications. We offer scholarly as well as popular publications; there are works of fiction along with books that draw from all the arts and sciences of our civilization. These books afford readers a rich source of the enduring wisdom of mankind.

Sophia Institute Press is the publishing arm of the Thomas More College of Liberal Arts and Holy Spirit College. Both colleges are dedicated to providing university-level education in the Western tradition under the guiding light of Catholic teaching.

If you know a young person who might be interested in the ideas found in this book, share it. If you know a young person seeking a college that takes seriously the adventure of learning and the quest for truth, bring our institutions to his attention.

www.SophiaInstitute.com
www.ThomasMoreCollege.edu
www.HolySpiritCollege.org

SOPHIA INSTITUTE PRESS

THE PUBLISHING DIVISION OF

Sophia Institute Press® is a registered trademark of Sophia Institute. Sophia Institute is a tax-exempt institution as defined by the Internal Revenue Code, Section 501(c)(3). Tax I.D. 22-2548708.